Hiram Calkins, De Witt Van Buren

Biographical Sketches of John T. Hoffman and Allen C. Beach

Hiram Calkins, De Witt Van Buren

Biographical Sketches of John T. Hoffman and Allen C. Beach

ISBN/EAN: 9783743352223

Manufactured in Europe, USA, Canada, Australia, Japa

Cover: Foto ©Raphael Reischuk / pixelio.de

Manufactured and distributed by brebook publishing software
(www.brebook.com)

Hiram Calkins, De Witt Van Buren

Biographical Sketches of John T. Hoffman and Allen C. Beach

BIOGRAPHICAL SKETCHES

OF

JOHN T. HOFFMAN

AND

ALLEN C. BEACH,

THE

DEMOCRATIC NOMINEES FOR GOVERNOR AND LIEUTENANT-GOVERNOR OF THE STATE OF NEW YORK.

ALSO,

A RECORD OF THE EVENTS IN THE LIVES OF OLIVER BASCOM, DAVID B. McNEIL, AND EDWIN O. PERRIN, THE OTHER CANDIDATES ON THE SAME TICKET.

BY

HIRAM CALKINS AND DE WITT VAN BUREN.

———— ·•·· ——— — —

NEW YORK:

THE NEW YORK PRINTING COMPANY.

81, 83, AND 85 CENTRE STREET.

1868.

CONTENTS

ERRATA.

Two or three technical errors have been overlooked in the haste of arranging the documents for the Sketches.

On page 8, it should read "New York," instead of "White Plains."

On page 51, "in and about," instead of "inside."

On page 59, should read "acts and deeds," instead of "actual deeds."

On page 79, in speech, "the nomination of President," should read "the assassination of the President."

On page 97, should read "Miss" Pickering, instead of "Mrs."

JOHN T. HOFFMAN.

CHAPTER I.

HOFFMAN'S EARLY LIFE.

THE name of HOFFMAN has long been familiar to every Democrat in this State. It is a name which has for a quarter of a century, at least, been associated with the traditions, identified with the history, the growth of our State, and the struggles of the Democratic party. On almost every page of its history this name is to be found, and, like that of Seymour, occupies a foremost position on all occasions.

The branch of the Hoffman family from which the present nominee for Governor sprang is, however, more noted for its triumphs in scientific and professional walks of life, rather than in the political field. It has been as prominent in the social as the other branch has been in the political world, but with the present generation it bids fair to excel in its political triumphs also.

Philip Livingston Hoffman, the grandfather of the subject of our memoir, resided for a number of years in Columbia county of this State. He was educated to the law, but never devoted much of his time to that profession. At an early age he married Helena Kissam, who belonged to one of the most noted families in that section, and whose name will also be recognized as belonging to one of the oldest families of the city of New York. Here are linked the names and blood of the Livingstons, Hoffman, and Kissam. Thus were associated names not only illustrious, but which are remembered with affection by our oldest citizens, as among the most valuable members of early society, and the founders of many public charities and works of benevolence.

This union was blessed with three sons: Adrian Kissam Hoffman, father of the present Democratic nominee for Governor; Dr. Richard K. Hoffman, who was extensively known in his profession, and whose death six or seven years ago was universally lamented; and Charles O. Hoffman, for a long time member of the firm of Fellows, Hoffman & Co., well-known merchants of this city.

1

The father of the subject of this memoir was born while the family resided in Columbia county. They subsequently moved to Montgomery county. It was there that Adrian Kissam Hoffman commenced his studies, preparing himself for the medical profession. Having concluded his studies, and received his diploma, Dr. Hoffman married the daughter of Dr. Thompson, of Galway, Saratoga county, and entered upon the practice of medicine at Sing Sing, Westchester county. He soon became celebrated in his profession, and was widely known and universally respected, not only for his skill as a physician, but also for his character as a man.

On January 10th, 1828, was born their son, John Thompson Hoffman, the subject of our biography. One of his first instructors outside of his family was one of the Primes of the New York *Observer*. Soon after Mr. Hoffman's first election as Mayor, his first teacher published an article in the *Observer*, in which he alluded to him in the following language:—

"More than thirty years ago, I was teaching in the Academy at Sing Sing. We had pupils learning their letters and those fitting for college and business. Among the former was the lad who became Mayor of the City of New York on the first day of the present year, John T. Hoffman. He learned his letters and to read at my knee. * * * * * While yet a student he won some reputation as a public speaker. But his calm self-possession, independence of association, and deliberate judgment, with great firmness of adherence to conclusions reached after careful examination, were qualities so rarely developed in a young man that he early attracted attention as one in whom high trusts could be safely confided. * * * * I take no credit to myself for his career. The man at the head of the school, my father, had exalted ideas of justice, and inculcated in his daily instructions those notions of stern integrity, the inflexibility of principle, the abstract duty of doing right irrespective of expediency, that go to make up the character of every really great man."

Under these teachings and under such examples the boyhood of John T. Hoffman was spent until he was ready to enter college. He showed that he possessed a studious mind, in fact that it was too vigorous for his body. The result was that he was retarded in his studies, and on two or three occasions obliged to abandon his books and forget his tasks until he could strengthen his body. But in spite of these disadvantages he made rapid advancement, and won many flattering prizes at the academy in his native town.

In the fall of 1843 he entered Union College, at Schenectady, as a member of the junior class. Here he again applied himself with all his characteristic industry, and grappled with the increased studies that were heaped upon him with all the vigor that marked his preliminary course. The exertion was too great, and he found himself obliged during the following year to relinquish his studies for a time and devote himself to recuperating his health and strength. Under the advice of physicians he entirely abandoned his books for a year.

Early in the autumn of 1845 he re-entered college greatly improved in health. With close application and his usual industry, he soon overtook those who had been pushing forward during his temporary withdrawal. His career at college was a successful one, taking front rank among his fellow-students, not only in his studies but also as an orator. His success in all these particulars was fully equal to the most sanguine expectations of his friends. He, in fact, displayed, while in college, great self-possession, firmness, and adherence to conclusions reached, and graduated with high honors in 1846.

Soon after leaving college, Mr. Hoffman entered the law office of Gen. Aaron Ward and Judge Albert Lockwood, at Sing Sing, and there commenced the study of law. The exciting political events of that day attracted his attention to politics; while the struggles which were then taking place between the Hunkers and Barnburners, the Hards and Softs in the Democratic party, were carefully examined by him. During each campaign he was found on the stump in his native place, advocating the cause of the Democracy. His affiliations were with the Hunker, or Hard Shell, wing. In 1848, when he was but twenty years of age, he was placed on the State Central Committee of one of the Democratic factions, then called the Hard Shell Democracy. An address was issued by this committee which attracted considerable attention for the ability in which the questions at issue were handled. Mr. Hoffman on this, as on all other occasions, advocated adherence to the nominations of the party, and although not a voter, spoke in favor of the election of Lewis Cass for President and Chancellor Walworth and Charles O'Conor on the State ticket.

On the 10th day of January, 1849, his twenty-first birth-day, he was admitted to the bar, and commenced immediately to practise his profession.

During the following October he removed to the city of New York, and soon after entered into a law partnership with the late Samuel M. Woodruff and William H. Leonard, the firm name being Woodruff, Leonard & Hoffman, office in Wall street. The same industrious habits that marked his course while a student were again developed in business, while his eminent ability and marked probity in all his dealings soon drew to him a large practice, and at the same time secured the confidence of those who sought his assistance or counsel.

His first connection with politics in this city was with the Young Men's Tammany Hall Committee. He connected himself with this committee about 1854, and was one of its most active members. He became a member of Tammany Society in 1857, and two or three years later was selected member of Tammany General Committee. His connection with Tammany Hall, therefore, took place at the very period when its struggles were the greatest and the feuds the most bitter. He was there to witness the struggle for the control of that organization between Fernando Wood, Lorenzo Shepherd, and Isaac Fowler, the squabble between the Small and the Savage Committee for regularity, the Witter Committee, the Cooper Committee, and the Westchesterites, all names familiar to those who took part in political affairs at that time; but he did not become prominent in the organization, except as a member of the Young Men's Committee, until after Fernando Wood had seceded from Tammany and set up political business for himself by organizing Mozart Hall.

Mr. Hoffman had gained such prominence as a lawyer, as well as in the councils of the Democracy, that in the latter part of the year 1859 he was generally pressed for the important position of United States District Attorney. But President Buchanan could not be persuaded that Mr. Hoffman was not too young for the position of such importance. In the contest that ensued, Judge Roosevelt was appointed.

Mr. Hoffman was married in 1854 to a daughter of Henry Starkweather, one of the most respectable families of this city. He has one child, a girl of about fourteen summers.

He is a member of the Protestant Episcopal Church; attends at St. Ann's Church, in 18th Street, in which he was formerly a vestryman; is a man liberal in his religious views, and free from the fanatical conventionalities of the day.

CHAPTER II.

HIS CAREER AS RECORDER.

THE first office ever held by Mr. Hoffman was that of Recorder, the most responsible judicial office in the metropolis, to which he was elected in November, 1860.

This position he never sought, nor had he any idea that his name was to be presented to the convention until the morning of the day on which that body assembled. He was on that morning waited upon by a committee headed by Nelson J. Waterbury, and asked if he would accept the nomination of Recorder. He promised to give an answer at 3 o'clock that afternoon. Mr. Waterbury and associates returned at that hour, when Mr. Hoffman informed them that he could not be a candidate. They then asked if he would write a letter stating that fact. He replied that he had no objection; wrote the letter, and placed it in the hands of those gentlemen.

The convention assembled in Tammany Hall in the evening, and among the names presented for the nomination for Recorder were those of John T. Hoffman, Abraham D. Russel, Robert Livingston, and C. Bainbridge Smith. There were three ballots; the second being declared informal.

The vote on the first ballot stood :

John T. Hoffman,................ 45
Abraham D. Russel,.............. 65
Robert Livingston,.............. 17
C. Bainbridge Smith,............ 12

The second ballot being destroyed on some informality, it was never known how the vote stood, but on the third ballot John T. Hoffman received 108 votes, and Judge Russel 64 votes. His nomination was then made unanimous. The letter which he had written was not presented nor made known to the convention, nor any portion of it.

The first that Mr. Hoffman knew that he had been nominated was when he saw the announcement in the morning papers the next day. Upon the earnest solicitations of his friends, he finally concluded to accept the nomination. His principal opponent in the convention was subsequently nominated by Mozart Hall, and ran against Mr. Hoffman, while the Republicans placed in nomination Thomas B. Van Buren.

The vote on election-day stood as follows :

John T. Hoffman,............ 39,606
Abraham D. Russel,.......... 17,667
Thomas B. Van Buren,........ 36,110

Mr. Hoffman thus received over twenty-one thousand more than the Mozart candidate, and about four thousand more than the Republican nominee.

The striking peculiarity of this vote is more easily seen by comparing it with the votes for the other candidates on the same ticket; not one of the other Tammany candidates at that election was successful, except those who had an endorsement, and were nominated by some of the other Democratic factions; Mr. Hoffman was the only candidate of Tammany who succeeded without the assistance of outside organizations. This shows that he was at that day stronger than Tammany.

In the office of Recorder he conducted himself with dignity, impartiality, and tact, and at once took a high and honorable position. No person ever filled that office with such universal satisfaction as did Mr. Hoffman. The high order of his ability, and his eminent qualifications for that office, at once became manifest. None so young had ever been selected to discharge its duties, and not one made a more distinct and enviable impression upon the public mind. He proved in all respects a just judge; upright, inflexible, calm, dignified, and conscientious in all his decisions. Never hasty in discharging that most important duty, administering justly our criminal law, but ever dignified, cool, and profoundly impressed with the responsibility of his position.

His unflinching devotion to the aims of justice won him the esteem of all law-abiding citizens, irrespective of party. No previous Recorder brought to the discharge of his high official duties more strength of character, breadth of intellect, profound legal knowledge, and steady determination of purpose, than John T. Hoffman. His charges to juries, and his sentences to criminals, are of a higher stamp than the usual utterances of most of our judicial officers on such occasions. There is a strong religious sense of right about them; and they also carry along with them the duty of upholding law and order, and vindicating the majesty of the former. His remarks on such occasions were always marked with the delicate touches of humanity that belong to a person of sound mind and possessing a kind heart. They have about them all the true ring of the fearless, incorrupt, and upright judge.

During his first term as Recorder, Judge Hoffman delivered several important opinions regarding the rights of citizens and the welfare of communities. One of the most important of these is embodied in a charge to the Grand Jury of the Court of General Sessions at White Plains, Westchester county, December 22, 1862. The charge was prompted by the reported violation of the State laws against kidnapping. It is a most emphatic and incisive opinion against the infamous system of arbitrary arrests adopted by the Government during the war, and is substantially as follows:—

CORT OF GENERAL SESSIONS—BEFORE RECORDER HOFFMAN.

The Grand Jury of this Court were sworn in on Monday morning, James W. Underhill, foreman. Previous to his Honor's charging the jury, Mr. District Attorney Hall requested the Recorder to call special attention to kidnapping and abduction. Mr. Hall remarked that a number of complaints of this nature had been filed in his office. After some preliminary remarks upon the ordinary topics to which the Court is required to call the attention of the Grand Inquest, Recorder Hoffman made the following important observations upon illegal arrests, which will be read with interest by every citizen of this State :

At the close of the last week the District Attorney requested me in my charge to you to-day to give you special instructions in relation to the laws of this State against kidnapping. He intimated to me that cases had been brought to his notice in which it was alleged these laws had been violated, and which he would probably feel bound to submit to you for your consideration and action. Having repeated that request to-day, I deem it my duty to give you the desired instructions, and I shall do so briefly and yet pointedly. It is so generally reported and believed that for many months past numbers of persons have, without any lawful authority, been seized on and removed from this State against their will, that great importance attaches to the subject under consideration. At the same time it is so generally understood that these seizures and removals have been made under some claim or pretence of lawful authority that it becomes necessary to define and state the law with care, so that all who will may understand it.

That law, as I shall now state it, will, I think, commend itself to the good sense of all those who will examine it with unbiassed judgment, and will be the law of this court while I preside in it, until reversed, if reversed it ever shall be, by some higher tribunal. The Constitution of the United States, and the Constitution of the State of New York, have guaranteed to all citizens the security of their persons against unlawful seizures, and the laws of this State have in substance declared that whoever shall violate this constitutional guarantee shall be deemed guilty of a felony. The statute provides (vide Revised Statutes, 5th edition, vol. 3, page 943, section 30) as follows, viz. : Every person who shall, without lawful authority, forcibly seize and confine any other, or shall inveigle or kidnap any other, with intent either :

1. To cause such other person to be secretly confined or imprisoned in this State against his will ; or

2. To cause such other person to be sent out of the State against his will ; or

3. To cause such other person to be sold as a slave, or in any way held to service against his will, shall, upon conviction, be punished by imprisonment in the State Prison, not exceeding ten years.

Whoever within this State arrests a person charged with an offence alleged to have been committed therein against the laws, either of the State or of the United States, is bound to convey the person so arrested, without delay, before the proper magistrate or other judicial officer within the State, to be dealt with according to law. Any seizure of the person of a citizen for any other purpose is without lawful authority, and any detention or confinement of a person so arrested, for any longer time than may reasonably be required to convey him before such magistrate or officer, is also without authority of law.

The removal of any person from this State into any other State or Territory, to answer to any charge of having committed here an offence against the laws of either the United States or the State, is without authority of law ; and every person, whether he be an officer or private individual, who shall seize and confine any person whomsoever, charged with having committed any crime within the State, with intent either secretly to confine or imprison him here, or to remove him out of the State against his will, acts in violation of the statute I have just read to you, and renders himself liable to indictment and imprisonment. Upon the trial of such indictment, the fact that such seizure, confinement and removal was by order of the President of the United States, of any member of his Cabinet, or other officer of the Government, will constitute no legal defence. Neither the President, nor any member of the Cabinet, or other officer (not judicial), has any lawful authority to order the seizure, or imprisonment, or removal from the State of any citizen of the State for any offence whatever committed, or alleged to have been committed, within its borders. I need hardly add that the arrest and imprisonment of any person not charged with any crime, no matter by whom, or by whose order the same is made, is in violation of the Constitution and the law. The Constitution of the United States declares that in criminal prosecutions the accused shall have a speedy trial by jury in the State or district where the crime shall have been committed; and the seizure of any person, and his removal against his will from his State or district, is in violation of this provision of the Constitution, and, in the eye of our statute, without "lawful authority." There are constitutional and statutory provisions in relation to fugitives from justice. When an offence has been committed, or is alleged to have been committed, in another State, and when the offender has fled into this State, provision has been made by act of Congress, in conformity with and obedience to constitutional requirements, for his arrest and return to the State from which he has escaped. In such cases the Government of the State in which the offence is alleged to have been committed may make a requisition upon the Governor of this State, accompanied by the necessary proofs; and upon such requisitions the Governor of this State may issue his warrant for the arrest of the fugitive, by virtue of which he may be seized and returned to the jurisdiction from which he has fled.

In this way, and in no other, can he be lawfully seized and conveyed out of the State. Any person, whether he be an officer or not, who shall seize and imprison an alleged fugitive from justice (except to await a requisition), acts without lawful authority; and if he shall seize and detain him against his will, with intent secretly to imprison him here, or to remove him out of the State against his will, except upon such requisition and warrant, he is guilty of a violation of the statute I have read to you, and is liable to indictment and imprisonment. Upon trial of indictment the fact that he acted by order of the President, or of the Government, will constitute no legal defence. These, gentlemen, are plain propositions of law, which cannot be disputed, applicable to our loyal State, in which the State Courts are in almost uninterrupted session, in which judges and magistrates are faithful to their oaths to support the Constitution of the State and the Constitution of the United States, in which the laws are ample for the punishment of all offenders as well as the protection of all citizens—a State in which the Federal Courts are in session, with all their machinery in full operation, their judges and marshals and deputies ready to perform their duties, whose process can always be enforced, and whose judgments and decrees can always be executed—a State in which the acts of Congress are never resisted, and whose people venerate and respect the Constitution and the laws. In such a State, so circumstanced, not being the scene of actual military operations, not even an army within its borders, nor even any soldiery, excepting such as may be on their way to fight the battles of the Constitution and the Union, whose laws are not obstructed nor defied; where no form of the "law martial" can, by any construction, be made applicable to any person not mustered into "military service," it is my duty, as a judge, to declare to you that the seizure of her citizens, their secret imprisonment against their will, their removal from beyond her borders, without authority of law, to answer to criminal or other charges, their confinement in places beyond the reach of legal process, is in violation of the rights secured to them by the Constitution and by the laws, and it is the right and solemn duty of the Grand Jury to indict any person or persons who have in these respects offended against the law. I have now, gentlemen, discharged my duty. I leave you, under the obligations of your solemn oath, to the performance of yours. It may not be possible, to prevent entirely the arbitrary and unlawful seizure and removal of the citizens of our State; but it is possible to convict and punish those who in this respect shall be found guilty of a violation of our laws.

But the most important official act of Judge Hoffman, during his career as Recorder, was manifestly his charge to the Grand Jury in the Court of General Sessions in the case of the July rioters, delivered August 4, 1863. The story of those terrible days is too familiar to people in this city and State to require repetition. Retributive justice, with quick and certain footsteps, overtook the authors of that terrible mischief. Through the industry and perseverance of District Attorney Hall, the leading actors in the bloody scenes of the July riots were arrested, and their cases brought before the Grand Jury. The Recorder's charge to that body was one of the wisest, most fearless, conscientious, and dignified judicial warnings ever uttered by a public judge. Its high character and convincing justice were at once commended by all respectable classes, regardless of party opinions. Republican presses and Republican orators vied in extolling the conduct of Recorder Hoffman as in the highest degree praiseworthy. A Republican clergyman (Dr. Osgood), in his Sabbath pulpit, thanked "God for the honesty of purpose and high-toned justice which actuated Judge Hoffman," and declared it to be "a great consolation to us to know that there is such a man to administer justice among us."

This charge indisputably proves the law-abiding and order-loving qualities possessed by John T. Hoffman. It also proves that he is fully equal to an emergency requiring so much firmness and wisdom as did the prosecution of the July rioters. Below, the charge is presented in full, its great importance and appropriateness forming the only excuse for republishing a document of such length:

GENTLEMEN OF THE GRAND JURY.—The solemn and impressive oath which has just been administered to you indicates, and clearly, the duties which the law devolves upon you, and the manner and spirit in which you are expected to discharge them. I trust each one of you fully appreciates the responsibility of his position—never greater than at the present time; and I ask your careful attention to a few suggestions which, in obedience to the requirements of the law, as well as the necessities of the occasion, I feel bound to make. When you retire to the Grand Jury room, your first duty will be to perfect your organization by the selection of one of your number as clerk, whose duty it will be to keep a brief record of all your proceedings. Having done this, you will proceed promptly and industriously to investigate all cases of crime which have occurred within the jurisdiction of this court, and which may be brought to your knowledge.

It is made my duty by law to call your attention specially to all offences against the Excise and Usury laws, the laws passed to preserve the purity of elections, the laws forbidding lotteries and the taking of illegal fees by public officers, and the law passed in 1860, to prevent frauds in the sale of tickets upon steamboats and other vessels. It is also my duty to inform you that it is a misdemeanor for any Grand Juror or officer of the court to disclose the fact of an indictment having been found for felony against any person not in actual confinement, until such person shall be arrested. In a great city like this, gentlemen, crime always abounds, and criminals of every grade and degree are always to be found. With the exception of several minor offences, no crime can be punished, no criminal can be brought to justice and to judgment, without the preliminary action of the Grand Jury. You stand between the prisoner and the State, and it is for you to see that impartial justice is done to each.

The court opens this month, gentlemen, with an unusual large calendar. For a short period succeeding the commencement of the present war, the number of crimes committed in this city was very materially diminished; the prisons were less crowded, and the business of this court was less burdensome than usual. This state of things was attributable to various causes; but it was manifest to my mind that it would be but temporary. So it has been. For some months past crime has been on the increase—offences against the person and offences against property rivalling each other in frequency. Beyond all this, a general spirit of lawlessness has been spreading through the community. One of the worst signs of the times has been the prevalent disregard of, and want of respect for, the laws and the lawfully-constituted authorities. Dangerous men—dangerous because powerful and influential—have by example and precept taught the people to disregard and disobey constitutional and legal obligations, and, sometimes upon one pretext and sometimes upon another, have countenanced (if they have not counselled) disobedience and resistance. They have aimed their shafts not only at legislative enactments and constitutional provisions, but at the officers of the law—the judges of the land and the decisions of the courts. As in time of war every man becomes a military critic, and sits in judgment upon the operations of our army and the plans of a campaign, so every one has become an expounder of the Constitution and the laws, and assumes to sit in judgment upon the judicial tribunals of the State and nation. The people have become accustomed to look upon Constitutions and laws and authorities as less sacred than in earlier days they had been taught to believe they were. The pulpit and press, the political platform and Senate chamber, the social circle, and perhaps even sometimes the courts themselves, have been the schools in which these pernicious lessons have been taught. Manifestations of popular violence, sometimes in one direction and sometimes in another—sometimes against men of one set of opinions, and sometimes against those of another—have from time to time occurred in this city and elsewhere. When applauded, they have been applauded loudly; when condemned, they have been condemned feebly. Now one set of partisans and now another have spoken of them as " just outbreaks of popular indignation," or "patriotic uprisings of the people." Conservatives and prudent men have watched the growth of this evil with alarm, and foreseen and dreaded the harvest. They saw that it was in violation of and in hostility to the fundamental principles upon which all government and all society rest. They have sought to remind those in authority, and those having influence, that it was their solemn duty to inspire the people with respect for all law by never deviating from it themselves, and to make the people understand that obedience to law was the first duty of the citizen. They have proclaimed that, as there was no safety for the nation except in a faithful adherence to the Constitution, so there was no security for the people but in unbending respect for and obedience to the laws and the authorities of the land. Warning the legislative power of the State and nation against the enactment of unconstitutional laws, they have insisted and ever will insist that the courts, and not the people, are to sit in judgment upon the constitutionality of an act, and that, until declared by the courts to be unconstitutional, resistance to it by force and violence is criminal.

These warnings have not been heeded. The evil teachings of misguided and wicked men have not been without their effect; they have taken deep root in the popular mind. Infidelity to constitutional and legal obligations has produced its brood of evils. This infidelity, and the false teachings and examples of partisans of various sects and parties—aided as they have been by causes and elements which are always actively at work in times of war and civil convulsions—urged on by the spirit of lawlessness which they have created, have recently produced in this city an outbreak which resulted in violence and enormities without a parallel in the history of the country. The immediate cause of this was opposition to the enforcement of the conscription law; but this cause would have been wholly inadequate to the result, if the poison of constitutional and loyal infidelity and of false teaching and pernicious example had not been infused into the popular mind. The outbreak was fearful—its results dreadful. Whatever may have been the cause, and whoever may have been responsible for the terrible consequences, one thing is certain: the plea of resistance to the draft affords no justification or excuse, and it is the duty of every public officer and every private citizen to labor with all his strength to bring to justice and to judgment the men who have violated all law, outraged all decency, and trampled upon all rights. It is very clear that the mob, originating as it did with the single object of resisting the draft, soon came under the control of ruffians and outlaws. Those who first participated in it probably did not contemplate the results which followed. Yet they were inevitable. The elements of every mob, no matter what may be its original object or design, are anarchy and ruin; and the one which has so lately disgraced this city has given evidence of this by putting in peril the lives and property of innocent people, by burning orphan asylums, burning and plundering private residences, sacking stores and warehouses, robbing citizens upon the public streets, and committing murders too horrible to record.

Can the plea of resistance to the draft afford any excuse for such enormities as these? Do not those who entered upon those scenes of violence, with no other object than to destroy enrolments and delay the execution of a law to the provisions of which they were opposed, shudder at the results which they have been instrumental in producing? Can one honest man be found in this community who, after the experience of the last few weeks, does not in his heart condemn, this day, the whole theory of violent resistance to law? Does not every man in this great city, high or low, rich or poor, this day realize, with ten times more force than ever before, that this appeal shall be to the courts—not to violence—that there is no safety for the citizen or the State but in a rigid obedience to the laws, in a profound respect for the constituted authorities of the land, and in a determined maintenance and preservation of order and public peace, at all times, under all circumstances, and at all hazards—and that without all these there is no security for home or family, property or life? You must pardon me, gentlemen, for detaining you so long.

I have made these suggestions with a definite object and purpose. I trust they may not be wholly without effect. Whatever we may be able to do as individuals in allaying popular irritation, and in removing or counteracting, as far as may be just and proper, the causes which produce it, let us unite in doing with all the ability we possess. We stand here, however, to-day, not as individuals, but as public officers, charged with grave responsibilities. Let us not shrink from them. Let us remember that we are not partisans, but sworn officers of the law, determined at all hazards to enforce the law and preserve order, to protect the innocent and to punish the guilty. It is our duty to teach all men that those who burn asylums and houses and stores are guilty of arson, and shall be punished for that offence; that those who plunder and appropriate to themselves other men's goods upon the highways or elsewhere, with or without violence, as the case may be, become subject to and will suffer the penalties affixed to the crime of robbery or larceny; that a rioter is an enemy of society and an offender against the law, and that the punishment for murder is death. Doing this, we shall be discharging our public duties; failing to do it, we shall be false to our consciences and our oaths.

Gentlemen, the prisons are full of persons charged with crime. I call upon you to examine every case fearlessly, fairly, and impartially; let no prejudice or passion influence you; deal honestly, do justly. Be especially cautious in considering evidence of identity; upon this point mistakes may easily be made. Every man is presumed innocent until proved guilty. In our determination to do prompt and speedy justice, let us earnestly strive that no injustice shall be done. However excited and violent others may be, we must be cool and careful. Let us bring no disrespect upon the law or the courts by either too much or too little zeal. In maintaining law, let us not trample upon it; in sustaining justice, let us not violate it. When you have presented to this court indictments against those whom you believe to be guilty, they shall be brought to a speedy trial before a petit jury, and, if convicted, shall be promptly sentenced to suffer the penalties of the law.

In conclusion, let me say, we have no time to be idle. Every consideration demands that all of us should work diligently. The press of business is great. I must urge upon you to remain in session as many hours each day as the District Attorney may desire. Personal convenience must yield to public necessity, and public necessity demands of you and of me and of every officer of the Court untiring labor and devotion. Let us, therefore, labor diligently, each in his proper sphere striving to do all he can toward preserving the public peace, restoring the public confidence, and meting out prompt and speedy justice to all offenders against the laws.

Delivered Aug. 4, 1863.

It was during this term that his firm decisions in reference to the low order of concert saloons secured for him the endorsement of the public generally.

On the 25th of June, 1862, Recorder Hoffman rendered a decision in a case where indictment had been made for publicly keeping spiritous liquors for sale on Sunday. In his decision he narrowed the argument to two considerations, viz., whether under the law of 1860 the "publicly keeping" of liquors on Sunday is made a misdemeanor, and whether the facts specially alleged constituted in law such public keeping. The Recorder elaborately reviewed both the law and the facts, and concluded that there was nothing in the law of 1860 expressive of an intent to make violation of the clause relating to Sunday observance a criminal offence.   Concerning the second consideration, that was beyond his jurisdiction, and a question for the civil courts.

CHAPTER III.

RE-ELECTION AS RECORDER, AND HIS SECOND TERM.

THE course of Mr. Hoffman as Recorder drew to him the universal approbation of the public without regard to parties.   Before the close of his term, or on the 12th of October, 1863, the Republican Judiciary Convention of this city assembled to make nominations for the several judicial offices to be filled at the election that fall.   When the office of Recorder was reached, Charles S. Spencer's name was presented as a candidate.   Mr. Spencer immediately withdrew his name, and in a speech eulogizing Mr. Hoffman, he declared him " one of the purest, ablest, and one of the most upright and conscientious public officials that was ever elected to an office in this city."

Other speeches were made by Republicans present, endorsing Mr. Hoffman in equally strong terms, when he was nominated by acclamation.   The following committee was appointed to notify him of his nomination: John Sedgwick, Waldo Hutchings, John H. White, Ira O. Miller, Guy R. Pelton, and Frederick Olmstead; all prominent in that party.

In discharging this duty, the committee addressed Mr. Hoffman the following letter:—

UNION HEADQUARTERS, No. 630 BROADWAY, }
New York, October 22, 1863. }

SIR:—The undersigned have been appointed a committee by the Union Judiciary Convention, to inform you that on the 1st instant you were unanimously nominated by that Convention as its candidate for Recorder of the City of New York.

The committee were instructed further to declare, that the nomination was made for the reasons that your judicial judgments have been impartial and uninfluenced by partisan considerations; that the manner in which you have performed your official duty demands your re-election, and that you have been neither doubting nor cold in the support of the national cause.

We have the honor to be, your obedient servants,

> JOHN SEDGWICK, Chairman.
> WALDO HUTCHINGS.
> JOHN H. WHITE.
> IRA O. MILLER.
> GUY R. PELTON.
> FREDERICK OLMSTEAD.

To the HON. JOHN T. HOFFMAN.

The week following his nomination by the Republican convention, the Tammany Hall and Mozart conventions both met, and also nominated him. This secured to him the endorsement of every convention and party, except a small faction known as the McKeonites. On election-day he received 60,000 votes out of the 64,000 polled for that office. This was a tribute of respect and confidence such as never before was shown to any official, and proves conclusively that his official conduct during his first term was universally endorsed throughout the city.

This marked approval on the part of the people, would in most cases have caused egotism on the part of the recipient almost unendurable. But it had no such effect upon Mr. Hoffman. He looked upon it simply as an approval by the people of conscientious acts. In conversation with him about this time, we remarked " that he had made a lucky hit, and secured both fame and popularity at a very early age." To this he replied, " It is a very easy matter to obtain both. All that is necessary is for a man to conscientiously do his duty, and not allow himself to be swerved from what is right and just, and he will find that popularity and fame come of itself."

His second term as Recorder was characterized by the same unswerving devotion to his duties, to justice, and the administration of the laws, as well as the same singleness of purpose in upholding the interests of the city, as that which marked his previous term.

One of the most important features of this term was his opinion in the Arguelles case. Robert Murray, United States Marshal, and others, had been indicted by the Grand Jury for the forcible seizure and confinement of Arguelles, in violation of the laws of the State against kidnapping. The case attracting attention in all parts of the country, an effort was made to take it out of the State and city courts, and transfer it to the United States court. Mr. Hoffman's opinion, denying the motion to transfer the jurisdiction of this case to the United States court, contains several logical conclusions upon the rights of the people and of States that have peculiar significance at this time.

HOFFMAN, Recorder.—The defendants have been indicted by the Grand Jury in and for the city and county of New York, for the forcible seizure and confinement of one Arguelles, in violation of the laws of the State of New York against kidnapping.

To this indictment no plea has been interposed by the defendants ; but under the provisions of section five of chapter eighty-four of the laws of the Thirty-seventh Congress, they have presented a petition to this Court, stating that the act complained of was done by order of the President of the United States, and asking for that reason that the indictment may be removed from this Court into the United States Circuit Court for trial.

Section 4, of the Act of Congress referred to, provides that any order of the . President, or under his authority, made at any time during the existence of the present rebellion, shall be a defence in all Courts to any action or prosecution, civil or criminal, for any search, seizure, arrest or imprisonment, made, done, or committed, or acts omitted to be done, under and by virtue of such order, etc., etc., and that such defence may be made by special plea or under the general issue ; and sec. 5 of the Act under which this application is made is as follows:

"Sec. 5. And be it further enacted, That if any suit or 'prosecution,' 'civil' or 'criminal,' has been or shall be commenced in any State Court against any officer, civil or military, or against any other person, for any arrest or imprisonment made, or other trespasses or 'wrongs' done or committed, or any act omitted to be done, at any time during the present rebellion, by virtue or under color of any authority derived from or exercised by or under the President of the United States, or any Act of Congress, and the defendant shall, at the time of entering his appearance in such Court, or if such appearance shall have been entered before the passage of this Act, then, at the next session of the Court in which such suit or 'prosecution' is pending, file a petition, stating the facts, and verified by affidavit, for the removal of the cause for trial at the next Circuit Court of the United States, to be holden in the district where the suit is pending, and offer good and sufficient surety for his filing in such Court, on the first day of its session, copies of such process and other proceedings against him, and also for his appearing in such Court, and entering special bail in the cause, if special bail was originally required therein. It shall then be the duty of the State Court to accept the surety and proceed no further in the cause or 'prosecution,' and the bail that shall have been originally taken shall be discharged. And such copies being filed, as aforesaid, in such Court of the United States, the cause shall proceed therein in the same manner as if it had been brought in said Court by original process, whatever may be the amount in dispute or the damages claimed, or whatever the citizenship of the parties, any former law to the contrary notwithstanding."

*   *   *   *   *   *   *   *   *

I will not now discuss the character of this most remarkable legislation. At the proper time, and in the proper place, it will, I trust, receive the consideration and construction which it merits. The question of its constitutionality, except so far as it affects the question of the transfer of the indictment to the courts of the United States, is not involved in this motion, and I shall not examine here any question but the one at issue. Upon the argument of the motion the counsel for the defendant asserted that if the indictment should be removed to the United States Circuit Court, and a trial should be there had, followed by a conviction, that the Judge of the United States Court could sentence the defendant under the laws of the State of New York to suffer the punishment prescribed by those laws, and that the power to pardon would rest in the President of the United States.

If these assertions were well founded we should have the strange picture presented of a United States judge administering the penal laws of the State of New York, and the President of the United States extending a pardon to one convicted of a crime against the laws of that State, which had been committed by his own order. Such a result would seem to be more appropriate to an act entitled "An act to prevent the punishment of any man who shall commit a crime by order of the President of the United States."

But I think these assertions of counsel are not well founded and cannot be maintained.

There is no authority for saying that a judge of a United States Court could sentence a criminal in pursuance of the laws of a State. Those judges have no powers except such as are conferred upon them by the laws of the United States, under the Constitution of the United States. Congress has never conferred upon them the power to pass any sentence upon any criminal offender against the laws of a State. Even the act of 1863 is wholly silent upon the subject, and no provision to that effect had ever been made before, because (if for no other reason) no one, until 1863, ever contemplated that a Court of the United States would ever be called upon to try offenders against the criminal laws of a State.

If then this indictment was transferred, and the defence that the act complained of was done by the order of the President of the United States should fall, and the defendant should be convicted, no judgment whatever could follow upon that conviction.

Again, if a judgment could follow, no pardon could be extended to the offender; the President of the United States could not pardon, for the reason that the offence is against the laws of the State, and not against the laws of the United States; and section two of article two of the Constitution of the United States confers upon the President the power to pardon and reprieve only for offences against the United States.

That it did not confer upon the President the power to pardon offenders against the laws of a State, if convicted in a United States Court, is, perhaps, a good argument to show that the framers of that Constitution never contemplated that an offender against the laws of a State should be tried in the Courts of the United States.

The Governor of the State of New York could not pardon, because this power under the Constitution of the State clearly relates only to cases of conviction in the Courts of the State. It is very clear the framers of that Constitution never contemplated that any other Courts would be clothed with power to enforce the State's penal laws.

Again, section 6 of the Act of Congress above mentioned provides that any suit or prosecution described in that act, in which final judgment may be rendered in the Circuit Court, may be carried by writ of error to the Supreme Court, whatever may be the amount of the judgment. The closing words of this section show that it relates only to civil suits or proceedings, and not to criminal, and it is the only provision on that subject in the act.

Now, it is well settled that the judgments of the United States Circuit Court in criminal cases are final, and the Supreme Court possesses no appellate jurisdiction in such cases. (U. S. v. Moore, 3 Cranch, 159; ex parte Kearney, 7 Wheaton, 38; ex parte Watkins, 3 Peters, 193.)

It is only in cases where the Circuit Judges are divided in opinion that the case can be brought before the Supreme Court (Act of April 29, 1802).

If, therefore, this indictment remains in this Court, and a question under the Act of Congress of 1863 shall arise, in the progress of the cause, the Supreme Court of the United States, in the exercise of its appellate jurisdiction, could ultimately review the judgment of this Court, and pass upon the constitutionality of the law in question.

If, on the other hand, it is transferred to the United States Circuit Court, the question of the constitutionality or unconstitutionality of the law of Congress cannot be submitted to the adjudication of the Supreme Court of the United States.

These suggestions are, in my judgment, material to the question under consideration, because they tend to show, in the first place, that, although the words of the Act of 1863 are very broad, yet Congress could hardly be considered to have intended (even if they had the power to do so) to confer jurisdiction upon the United States Court to try, in the first instance, an indictment found in a State Court, inasmuch as they have wholly neglected to provide any way in which that jurisdiction could be exercised, and on which the case could be prosecuted to judgment and execution. And inasmuch as the effect would be to deprive the Supreme Court of the appellate jurisdiction, in the exercise of which it could reverse the judgment of the State Court if the indictment was not removed.

In the second place, the suggestions tend to show that, even if Congress did so intend, it is not only an instance of legislation not contemplated by the Constitution of the United States, but is so improvident and incomplete that no Courts can give effect to it.

II. But, independent of these suggestions, Congress has no power, in my judgment, to confer upon the United States Court jurisdiction to try indictments found in the State Courts.

The case of Jones v. Seward, decided in the Supreme Court in this district, is no authority in this case. I need not pause to state the difference in the two cases. They are wholly unlike.

The argument of the defendant's counsel is, that, upon the trial of this indictment, the consideration of a law of the United States will be involved—that in every case arising under the laws of the United States the Courts of the United States have appellate jurisdiction to reverse the judgments of the State Courts, and that, in all cases to which this appellate jurisdiction extends, Congress has the power of conferring original jurisdiction. In support of this he quotes the *dictum* of Chief Justice Marshall, in the case of Osborn *v.* The United States (9 Wheaton's Reports, 821), which is as follows: "We perceive no grounds upon which the proposition can be maintained, that Congress is incapable of giving to the Circuit Court original jurisdiction in any case to which the appellate jurisdiction extends."

Whatever Chief Justice Marshall has said is entitled to the greatest respect, and I should hesitate about refusing to assent to it, if I could not issue a warrant for such refusal in his own recorded declarations. I do not find such warrant in his opinion in the case of Cohens *v.* Virginia (Wheaton's Reports, 264), in which he says: "It is a maxim not to be disregarded, that general expressions, in every opinion, are to be stated in connection with the case in which these expressions are used. If they go beyond the case they may be respected, but ought not to control the judgment in a subsequent suit, in which the very point is presented for decision."

2

Now, in the light of this maxim, I propose to show that what Chief Justice Marshall said in the case of Osborn has no application to and is no authority in the case now under consideration.

The Bank of the United States sued Osborn in the United States Circuit Court, by authority of its charter, which was under an act of Congress, and which gave the United States Courts original jurisdiction of suits by and against the bank. The Court decided that that provision in the charter was warranted by the third article in the Constitution, which declared that the judicial power of the United States should extend to all cases arising under the Constitution and "the laws of the United States." Judge Marshall said: "This suit is a case, and the question is, whether it arises under the laws of the United States;" and soon after he says: "The Constitution enumerates cases in which the jurisdiction of the United States Courts is original and exclusive, and then defines that which is appellate," and he adds as follows:

"It is not insinuated that the judicial power, in cases depending upon the character of the cause, cannot be exercised in the first instance in the Courts of the Union."

And then he uses the words cited by defendant's counsel, and soon after uses this all-important language:

"We think then, that when a question, to which the judicial power of the Union is extended, forms an ingredient in the original cause, it is in the power of Congress to give the Circuit Courts jurisdiction of that cause, although other questions of fact may be involved in it. The case of the bank is, we think, a very strong case of this description. The charter of incorporation not only creates it, but gives it every faculty it possesses."

"This being (meaning the bank) can acquire no right, make no contract, bring no suit, which is not authorized by a law of the United States."

"Can a being thus constituted have a case which does literally, as well as substantially, arise under this law?"

And in another place he says:

"The act itself is the first ingredient of the case—its origin."

It was under such a state of facts, and in such case, that Judge Marshall gave utterance to the dictum quoted by the defendant's counsel. It was applicable to such a case, and to every case where a question arising under an act of Congress is involved "in the character of the cause," "forms an ingredient of the original cause," exists in its very inception, and without the consideration of which the cause cannot proceed a single step.

It has no application to a case in the origin of which neither the Constitution or laws of the United States are involved, and in which a question involving action may never arise, or if it does, can only arise "in the progress of the cause."

In the case of Cohens v. Virginia, above cited, we find Chief Justice Marshall furnishing an authority upon this point, when he says, as follows:

"That the Constitution or a law of the United States is involved in a case, and makes a part of it, may appear in the progress of a cause in which the Courts of the Union, but for that circumstance, would have no jurisdiction, and which of consequence could not originate in the Supreme Court. In such a case the jurisdiction could only be exercised in the appellate form."

In the same case, Judge Marshall says: "The original jurisdiction of the Supreme Court, where a State is a party, refers to those cases in which jurisdiction might be exercised in consequence of the character of the party, and an original suit might be brought in any of the Federal Courts. Not to those cases in which the original suit might not be initiated in a Federal Court of the last description, in every case between a State and its citizens, and perhaps every case in which a State is enforcing its penal laws. In such cases, therefore, the Supreme Court cannot take original jurisdiction."

It needs no argument to show the application of these words of Judge Marshall to the case now under consideration—a case in which "the State of New York is seeking to enforce its penal laws," and which could not have been instituted in the Courts of the Union. A case in which a question under a law of the United States may never be presented at all, or, if it should be, can only be "in the progress of the cause." For an indictment by the People of the State of New York against one of its citizens for an offence against its penal laws does not involve in itself any question under any law of Congress. If such question should ever arise, it could only be on the progress of the defence. If it should then arise, and a decision should be adverse to the law, the Supreme Court of the United States would, in the exercise of its appellate jurisdiction, reverse the judgment of the State Courts. If it should not arise, then the Courts of the United States could have no jurisdiction at all.

The Recorder then proceeds to quote from eminent legal authorities to sustain his position, closing his opinion as follows :—

It is not enough that an Act of Congress gives the United States Circuit Court jurisdiction. It can have no jurisdiction which is not conferred by the Constitution, as well as the law.

The construction which I contend for is, I think, just and reasonable. It secures to the State all its rights, and it secures to the Federal Government all it needs, and all it has any right to demand. It secures to the State its right, in the first instance, to prosecute all offenders against its laws in its own Courts, and to insure them punishment in case of conviction.

It secures to the Federal Government the right to review, in its Supreme Court, the judgment of the State Courts in all cases where a defence to an indictment arises under an Act of Congress, if such defence should be overruled by the State Courts. If the judgment of the State Courts was erroneous, it would be reversed. If it was not, it would be affirmed, and the case would be remanded to the State Court for judgment.

On the other hand, the construction of the Constitution contended for by defendant's counsel would deprive the State Courts of all power and right to enforce the Federal laws of the State in all cases in which Congress should undertake to declare what should be a defence to them.

It would subject the penal laws of a State to the will of Congress. It would, under the Act in question, entitle any criminal indicted in our Courts for any offence to allege that he acted by order of the President, and to claim the removal of the cause into a Court of the United States. It would, as I have shown, transfer an indictment for any offence against a State law to a Court organized under a United States law, which has no power to enforce the laws of the State, or to punish in accordance therewith. If the defendant, upon such transfer, could be tried and convicted, it would place him in a position to which no power of pardon could extend ; and last, but not least, the transfer to the United States Circuit Court in the case now under consideration, or in any case like it, would prevent hereafter the consideration by the Supreme Court of the United States of the extraordinary Act of Congress under which this motion to transfer has been made.

Considerations such as these may have influenced Judge Marshall, when he, in the case of Cohens *v.* Virginia, used the language I have before quoted, and they may have also influenced Chief Justice McKean, when he declared in Respublica *v.* Cobbett (3 Dallas Reports, 476) " That neither the Constitution, nor the Act of Congress, ever contemplated that any Court under the United States should take cognizance of anything savoring of criminality against the State."

Believing, therefore, as I do, that the State of New York has the right, under the Constitution of the United States, to try in its Courts all offenders against its penal laws, subject to the right of the United States Supreme Court to review their judgments, if in the process of the trial a question should arise, under any law of the United States, and believing, as I do, that Congress has no power to deprive the State of New York of that right, I concur in the decision of Judge Russell denying the defendant's motion to transfer the indictment.

It was during this term that the case of Ketchum came before him. His last act as Recorder was the sentencing of this unfortunate man. Young Ketchum was arraigned on the 30th of December, 1865, for his sentence, having been previously convicted. A motion was made to stay proceedings, but this was denied ; whereupon Judge Hoffman delivered the following sentence :—

" I have given your case, Edward B. Ketchum, most anxious and careful consideration ; not because I ever doubted what the interests of society required or duty demanded of me, but for the reason that I well know that many gentlemen of high character and excellent judgment entertained views entirely at variance with my own. Occupying, as you did, an exalted position among the business men of this great commercial city ; commanding, as you did, unlimited confidence and credit ; possessed, as you were, of great wealth and influence, you became involved in speculations as vast as they were dangerous and ruinous ; and then, to save the financial ruin of yourself and house, which seemed imminent, you did what no one of inferior position or credit could have done, raised* immense sums of money upon paper which you forged, the genuineness of which no one doubted, simply because you presented it. It was the every-day story, varying only from other stories in the magnitude of the forgeries and the greatness of your fall, and you gave a shock to credit and to confidence from which the business interests of the city did not readily recover. Your friends and those who ask for you the mercy of the Court say you were laboring under a mania. But every man whose personal sympathies do not to some extent warp his judgment, knows that it was no other mania than that which seizes on every man who commits a crime in order to avert a personal calamity which he cannot endure to meet. If, sitting here as a judge, I should mitigate your punishment for any of the reasons assigned, or because hearts are aching and fainting, or because of my own personal sympathies with those who mourn for you, I should feel that every sentence I had passed upon a first offender had been a wrong, and that I was indeed a 'respecter of persons.' It is my duty so to administer the law that all men may feel and know that none are beyond either its protection or its power. It may well be, as claimed by your friends, that if you were permitted to go free, you would soon be able to redeem your reputation and re-establish your position. *But if this court should yield to their application, it would* *be an official declaration that men of influence and station could offend against the laws without the fear of punishment.* Public interests and necessities demand that the penalties of violated law should be visited upon the offender by way of example as well as of punishment. If you had been put upon trial upon all the indictments brought against you, the term of your imprisonment would have extended through the greater part of your life. The District Attorney has vindicated the law by arraigning you upon one to which you have pleaded guilty, with full knowledge of the consequences. Upon that plea the extreme punishment is five years' imprisonment. The law, however, directs that the term of imprisonment shall not expire during the winter months. In discharge, therefore, of my duty, I must pronounce the sentence of the Court, which is that you be imprisoned in the State Prison for the period of four years and six months."

It will be remembered that this was addressed to a person whose friends believed that from their wealth and position in society they could prevent that punishment which would be dealt out to one less fortunate in worldly goods. The most persistent and extraordinary efforts were made, and the strongest influence brought to bear, both to defer and to mitigate the sentence. But all this had no effect upon Judge Hoffman. He saw before him the path of duty, of justice, and right, and could not be swerved from it.

CHAPTER IV.

HIS NOMINATION AND FIRST ELECTION AS MAYOR.

THE contest for Mayor in New York in the fall of 1865 was one of the most exciting that has ever taken place in this city. It was a contest in which the leading Republicans throughout the country took more interest than any which had taken place for years. Before the close of the State campaign that year, the Citizens' Association had placed John Hecker in the field as its candidate. Immediately after the November election, the *Tribune* came out in support of Mr. Hecker, and urged his endorsement by the Republicans. C. Godfrey Gunther, whose term was about expiring, announced himself as a candidate, and was nominated for re-election by the faction known as the McKeon Democracy.

The Republicans, failing to be convinced by the arguments of the *Tribune* that it was their duty to nominate Mr. Hecker, met in convention, and, after considerable parleying, placed in nomination

Marshall O. Roberts, and entered upon the canvass prepared to spend a small fortune to elect him.

While these steps were being taken by those factions, an effort was made to unite Tammany and Mozart Halls upon one candidate. The conventions of both of those organizations assembled and appointed a committee of conference, and then adjourned one day to await their report. On the 21st of November these committees made their respective reports. It was found that it was impossible for Tammany to unite with Mozart Hall except upon an agreement to take Fernando Wood as the candidate. Tammany, having just gone through a contest at the State Convention with Wood in regard to regularity and won in the contest, was unwilling to surrender all gained there and now support Wood for Mayor.

The Tammany Committee, through Hon. John Kelly, reported that they were unable to agree, whereupon F. I. A. Boole stated, that it having been determined to make no alliance with Mozart, and that, from what he had seen and heard, he was satisfied that Hon. John T. Hoffman was the choice of the delegates comprising the convention, he would therefore move that he be nominated by acclamation. Several speeches were made, and a letter read from Elijah F. Purdy withdrawing his name, when a ballot was taken, and Mr. Hoffman received the unanimous vote of the convention.

Among the speeches made on this occasion was one by Hon. John Van Buren, who declared "the nomination of Mr. Hoffman was in every respect a wise one. That gentleman united in himself most extraordinary qualities, and he would be a worthy successor of the great men who have held the office of Mayor of the city of New York. Under his administration the million of souls in the metropolis would be protected in their legal rights."

The Mozart Convention assembled on the same day, nominated Fernando Wood, but that gentleman declined, whereupon the Convention endorsed John Hecker. The ball was then opened, and a bitter contest commenced. The Tammany ticket was Hoffman for Mayor and O'Gorman for Corporation Counsel. The Citizens' Association, Mozart Hall, and the *Tribune* labored for the election of John Hecker and Richard O'Gorman. The Republicans united upon Marshall O. Roberts, and were supported by the *Times* and the *Herald*. The lyrics of the campaign were far more numerous than in any previous canvass of the kind in the city. Not one of the principal papers in the city said a word against the character, the ability, and the fitness of Mr. Hoffman. It was, in fact, charged by some of the journals that he had been nominated by Tammany to give that organization respectability, and to save its reputation, as well as to prevent its overthrow. It was in this canvass that the *Herald* first called Mr.

Hoffman "Baron von Hoffman," and in a series of papers written in imitation of those popular articles of Gen. Halpine's, under the *sobriquet* of "Miles O'Reilly," endeavored to rally the Irish vote for Roberts, and create a jealousy between that class of our adopted citizens and the Germans.

The Republicans made a most desperate fight, spent money without stint, and, in fact, expended more money in the canvass than was ever used by all the candidates combined in any previous mayoralty election. The Citizens' Association also spent a small fortune trying to elect Hecker. The candidates were all men of high character and good standing in society. The race became therefore a spirited one. The *World*, *Journal of Commerce*, and the *Staats Zeitung* were the only daily papers that supported Hoffman. His high character—his honesty, his integrity and ability, however, compelled all the other papers to speak of him in eulogistic terms. The *Herald* was constrained to say that " Recorder Hoffman, a lawyer of unquestionable ability, large experience in city affairs, and known hostility to the associations of official plunderers, is well fitted for the position." The *Evening Post*, a Republican newspaper, expressed a decided preference for Mr. Hoffman. It said : "Hoffman seems to us to be preferred ; in talent, character, energy, he is like the old class of Mayors that we used to choose in the Willets, the Livingstons, the Coldens, the Clintons, and the Lees." The *Tribune* said : " Recorder Hoffman has a good reputation, which we would not tarnish." The New York *Times* declared Mr. Hoffman to be "a man of ability, energy, and integrity. He is known by all who know him at all, to be incapable of aiding or countenancing dishonesty in any official action, nor is he in the least likely to become the tool of cliques or individuals seeking personal profit at the expense of public good. As Recorder he has always been firm, upright, and courteous in the administration of justice, and in the riot trials of 1863 he evinced a fearlessness of popular clamor, and a high-toned devotion to justice and the public welfare, which entitle him to grateful remembrance from all who appreciate the perils which the city then barely escaped. His record during the war has been patriotic and loyal."

With such flattering assurances of popular regard as these, Mr. Hoffman went into the memorable mayoralty contest of 1865. The struggle was brief, but exciting and spirited. Mayor Hoffman's personal popularity, his patriotic record, and, above all, his great probity of character, decided the contest in his favor. The result of the election was as follows:—

Total votes.............................. 81,702
Hoffman.................................. 32,820
Roberts.................................. 31,657

Hecker 10,390
Gunther 6,758

Mayor Hoffman's first message to the Common Council, January 1, 1866, was characterized by its conscientious tone, its lucid exposition of the financial affairs of the city, and the excellence of its suggestions. One of the most important points of this message is contained in its pointed and excellent suggestion regarding a recodification of the charter, restoring to the city control of its own affairs, and clothing the Mayor with power commensurate with his responsibilities. We copy this clause :—

THE CITY AND ITS GOVERNMENT.

The growth and prosperity of this city are beyond parallel. Its resources are immense. Population and wealth are pouring into it from all parts of the world. The rich country which surrounds it contributes incessantly to its progress and advancement, and before many years the whole island on which it is situated will be crowded with an active and energetic people.

Such a city deserves and should have one of the best charters, and one of the strongest municipal governments which can be given by the legislative power of the State. What that charter should be, and what action the Legislature should take in reference to our local affairs, this is not the time to discuss; but in view of the present public agitation of that subject, I feel bound to state two propositions, which it is clear to me should never be lost sight of, and should be rigorously adhered to.

1. The city should be permitted to choose its own officers, carry on its own government, and manage its own affairs. Its chartered rights should be preserved, its privileges maintained, and never under any circumstances should the State Legislature attempt to saddle upon it a commission to govern and control it.

2. Its Mayor should be clothed with power commensurate with his responsibilities. A concentration of power and of responsibility should be the end and aim of all legislation relating to its government. It is the division of power and the division of responsibility which causes all or nearly all of our municipal evils, and the sooner this great truth is universally recognized and acted upon, the better for the common interests of us all.

One of the first of Mayor Hoffman's conspicuous acts after his election, was his veto message to the Common Council objecting to the resolution directing the Clerk of that body to take measures for the publication of 10,000 copies of the Corporation Manual.

The work, the Mayor thought, was useful, and the sum which it was proposed to pay Mr. Valentine for its compilation, $3,500, not excessive. But this little volume cost the year before over $57,000, or $5.70 each, while the Mayor believed, from careful inquiry, that it could be printed for $3.00 a copy. A large number of copies were given to city officials for distribution, and he saw no good reason why the privilege of such distribution should be bestowed upon the Mayor, the Common Council, and the Clerk, at a cost to the city of over

$50,000. Mayor Hoffman's action, however, was overridden by the Common Council, and the volume was printed as it had been in previous years.

Subsequently, in April, he vetoed two schemes aimed at the city treasury—one for an extra allowance to a contractor, and the other, resolutions authorizing a retired city inspector to continue to occupy rooms rented by the city, and keep an indefinite number of clerks for an indefinite time, to accomplish the unfinished business of his department.

These, together with similar acts, proved conclusively Mayor Hoffman's steady devotion to the people's interests, his unswerving integrity, his commendable strength of character and firmness of will. Although his powers were painfully circumscribed, and his official position hampered by the most provoking features of legislation, yet the Mayor managed, by dint of great perseverance, caution, energy, and the exercise of judicious foresight, to dignify his office, and make it at once an honor and an ornament to the city.

On the 13th of May, 1866, Mr. Hoffman delivered the address on the occasion of the inauguration of the monument erected in Greenwood by the Seventy-first Regiment, to the memory of Colonel Abraham S. Vosburgh. The oration abounded with scholarly allusions and effective eloquence. Its character may be judged by its peroration, which was as follows :

"We go hence in a few moments to the city of the living—the great scene of bustling, active life. Let us carry with us lasting recollections of this day, and resolve with renewed strength faithfully to discharge, in our respective spheres, our many duties as citizens of a country for the preservation of which our friend gave up his life. I would not intrude upon these serious reflections and solemn scenes, one political thought or one jarring sentiment ; but, standing beside the tomb, all of us, citizens and soldiers alike, may well express the earnest hope and prayer that the death of Vosburgh, and of the thousands of patriots and heroes who followed him, may not have been in vain ; that the Union and Constitution for which they died may be preserved and protected against all assaults ; that the States for the eternal union of which they perilled everything may not be kept asunder ; that fanaticism and madness everywhere may give way to a great and growing patriotism, which alone can make a people prosperous and happy ; that sectional prejudice, the rankest weed that ever grew in the garden of liberty, the intensest poison that ever polluted the wellspring of national prosperity, may be rooted out, and destroyed forever ; that the glories of peace and union shall indeed follow upon the horrors of civil war ; and that the whole people throughout the length and breadth of the land may be thoroughly inspired with the feeling that they have, and ever will have, 'one country, one Constitution, and one destiny.'"

When the obnoxious excise law went into effect, in the spring of 1866, a feeling of strong and bitter indignation prevailed throughout the city, in opposition to the despotic measure. On the 4th of June, the German citizens held a mass meeting in Union Square. Fully twenty thousand persons were present, and the occasion was marked by the adoption of most emphatic resolutions and the delivery of pronounced speeches. Mayor Hoffman wrote a letter to the meeting, which, like all his other public efforts, was characterized by dignity, force of statement, and breadth of view. The letter is as follows :—

MAYOR'S OFFICE, NEW YORK, June 2d, 1864.

GENTLEMEN :—I am in receipt of your invitation, to address a mass meeting of the German societies of New York, to be held in Union Square on Monday next.

I fully recognize your right to call upon me as a public man to express my sentiments upon a law which affects so many of my fellow-citizens, and I shall freely and fully declare them.

We all recognize the evils of intemperance, and the consequences to which the unrestrained sale of intoxicating liquors leads, and each of us should be willing to do his share to remedy these evils. You and I, and all citizens who have an interest in good government and the welfare of our fellow-men, look with approval upon any judicious and wholesome restraint in this direction. Any law which, while securing equal justice to all, shall, by proper regulations, deny licenses to disreputable persons, suppress disorderly houses and assemblages, and preserve order and decency throughout the community, demands and should receive an earnest support.

But I am as much opposed to intolerance as I am to intemperance, and a law which under the pretext of moral reform strikes at the life-long habits and customs of a large class of our people, which are as harmless as they are universal, will never be sustained by any considerable portion of our community. There is a spirit of intolerance in some of the provisions of the present law, against which you are right in remonstrating, and your remonstrances must be heard. A law which can be so construed as to enable officials to invade a man's house and home, and those clubs and associations which are legally as private as the home circle, which declares how long at night the lights may burn there, and at what hour those engaged in social intercourse there must cease their enjoyment and separate, and which follows with policemen and spies, and with restraint, large masses of the working population with their families, whenever and wherever they assemble, in accordance with life-long habits and customs, on their only day for rest and harmless recreation, creating no disorder and violating no man's rights, cannot receive my support as a wise and just exercise of legislation. Despotism is none the less oppressive because it comes in the form of law.

Parties and party principles are changing. There was a time, not remote, when the word "conservatism," as applied to the just rights and acknowledged liberties of the people, was the popular watchword of political parties. Now we have a powerful party boasting the name of "Radical," whose members take counsel in passion and legislate in our National and State halls with an aggressive vindictiveness which seems to recognize no limit, as if they were charged with a special mission to make all men's views conform to theirs.

I cannot better express my sentiments in regard to this class of reformers than by quoting the words of a distinguished statesman and orator, now gone, who at an early period foresaw the spirit of aggressive intolerance which was gaining ground among our public men.

He says: "There are men who, with clear perceptions, as they think, of their own duty, do not see how too eager a pursuit of one duty may involve them in violation of others, or how too warm an enhancement of one truth may lead to a disregard of others equally important; as I heard it strongly stated not many days ago, these persons are disposed to mount on a particular duty as upon a war-horse, and to ride furiously on and upon and over all other duties that may stand in the way. * * * If their perspicuous vision enables them to detect a spot on the face of the sun, they think that a good reason why the sun should be struck down from heaven. They prefer the chance of running into utter darkness to living in heavenly light, if that heavenly light be not absolutely without any imperfection. They are impatient men, too impatient always to give heed to the admonition of St. Paul, that we are not to do evil that good may come."

The limits of a letter will not permit the discussion of the law, and the principles it involves in its many aspects. But I have no hesitation in saying that as I understand the objects of your meeting, and to which I have alluded, they have my cordial sympathy and approval. But while the law in question remains on the statute-book, it is your duty, as good citizens, to obey it. You have already set an example of obedience to law which has secured to you the respect and sympathy of the public. Laws can only be avoided and set aside by the action of courts, or by the representatives of the people in Legislature assembled. One way to instruct those representatives is through the medium of powerful assemblages, in the mode adopted by you. Persistent vigilance in this legitimate direction will, I am confident, secure to you redress of the grievances of which you complain.

I am exceedingly obliged to you for the courtesy you have extended to me. But I think it desirable that your meeting should be addressed exclusively by your own speakers. I have stated to a member of your committee the reasons why I think so, and I need not repeat them here.

I am, gentlemen, very truly yours,

JOHN T. HOFFMAN.

On the 4th of July, 1866, the Tammany Society celebrated the recurrence of the National Anniversary with their customary fervor and patriotism. Mr. Hoffman, the Grand Sachem of the Order, delivered the following eloquent address:

BROTHERS AND FRIENDS: I welcome you heartily to this old wigwam, within which, for more than half a century, the Tammany Society has with unfailing regularity celebrated the anniversary of American independence. Its venerable walls bear the marks of time, and are blackened with the smoke of many a council-fire and many a conflict. In outward show it compares but poorly with the gilded temples of some more modern political associations; but in its ancient and honorable record—its glorious past and its bright future—it outshines them all. (Applause.) During the years of fearful struggle through which the nation has just passed, while other places, more elegant and more fashionable, were the resort of those who assumed to themselves much of the patriotism and loyalty of the land, Old Tammany was thrown wide open as a recruiting-place for a class of patriots who were willing to fight, as well as to talk, for their country. (Loud applause.) Brave men went forth from here who either died upon the battle-field or have returned, after an honorable discharge, to labor and to vote for the speedy restoration of that Union for the maintenance of which they hazarded their lives. Tammany Hall, true to its ancient record, never yielded to the demands of fanaticism or faltered in devotion to the Constitution (applause); and now that peace has come, it demands that with peace shall come "good-will to men." It sustained the war, as waged for the preservation of the Union and the Constitution, and having triumphed, it demands that neither the one nor the other shall be tampered with by politicians or fanatics, in Congress or out of it. (Applause.) On this anniversary of the Independence of the United States of America, it asserts, not as a theory but as a fact, that the States are united—that they are equal under the Constitution, and that the avowed determination of a Radical Congress to refuse representation to eleven of them, is a gross assumption and abuse of political power, which deserves to be and will be rebuked by an intelligent people. It demands, and will insist before the country, that the people of those eleven States, having abandoned the heresy of secession, and submitted to the authority of the Government, should have immediate representation in the persons of men who are true to the Constitution and the laws (applause), and that Radical partisans shall not, for the sake of perpetuating their political power, keep asunder those States, for the eternal union of which hundreds of thousands of brave men have perished, and thousands of millions of treasure have been expended. ("Never." Cheers.) In making these demands it is ready to start anew, in concert with conservative men everywhere, in a determined effort to overthrow those who, now that war is ended, will have no peace, and who, now that disunion is killed, will have no Union. (Cheers.) William D. Kennedy went forth the leader of a Tammany regiment, and died its representative. Before he went he joined with us in placing in front of the Old Wigwam Jackson's motto: "The Union, it must be preserved." Elijah F. Purdy, my immediate predecessor, in his proper sphere did noble service in the good cause, and died on the last anniversary of that great battle which gave to Jackson immortality. (Applause.) One by one the old braves have passed away, but the younger warriors retain their spirit and will vindicate their memories. They choose this day to start anew upon the war-path, and will not bury the tomahawk until all enemies of the Union of the States, and of the rights of the States, shall be overthrown. (Cheers.) The proprieties of the occasion, and the manifold exercises of the day, forbid a reference to great questions of national and State and local policy, which will at the proper time be discussed.

I again welcome you to the Old Wigwam. It may be the last time we shall assemble here. It is full of bright memories of the past and great hopes of the future; but it must soon give place to a new and more commodious one, which, in the greatness of its proportions and the harmony of all its parts, will be emblematical of the Union of which it is the representative. (Cheers.) Let a voice go forth from here to-day which will be heard throughout the land. (Cheers.)

CHAPTER V.

NOMINATION FOR GOVERNOR, AND THE CANVASS OF 1866.

As early as July, 1866, Mayor Hoffman's name began to be mentioned in the Democratic press of the State for the office of Governor.

His abilities as an executive officer, and the distinguishing probity of his official character, had attracted the attention of the Democracy of the State. He had, however, up to this time taken little or no part in State politics. While his fame as Recorder and Mayor of the City of New York had been sounded throughout the interior, yet he had but little personal acquaintance with the Democratic politicians of the State, and none with the masses of the party outside of New York and Brooklyn. The comments and eulogies of the city press were, however, echoed in the rural papers of the State. His speeches at the reception of President Johnson on his journey northward during that summer had been extensively published and read by the people. These had served to introduce his name and his abilities to circles where they had not been known before. Long before the Convention assembled, his name loomed up as one of the most prominent candidates for the position of Governor.

His strength began to be so universally conceded that the opposition press, under the lead of the *Herald* and *Tribune*, assailed him and endeavored to turn the tide in another direction.

The Convention assembled at Albany on the 11th day of September. It was a convention which was called under the joint auspices of the Democratic and Conservative Republican Committees; the latter having been appointed at a convention which previously assembled in Saratoga, to elect delegates to the Johnson National Convention. One-third of the Albany Convention was then Conservative Republicans. The Democracy of the State had just lost their great organizer, Dean Richmond, and during the election of delegates there was great anxiety as to who should be selected to fill his place. The convention was therefore an important gathering to the State, and on that account was looked upon with more than usual interest. The leading men of the Democracy were there, both those who had figured in its politics for years, as well as the young men of prominence who were just entering upon the stage of action. Many of the old wheel-horses of the Republican party were also in attendance, manifesting great anxiety as to the result.

As the delegates assembled it was found that there were numerous candidates for the nomination. Among these were Sanford E. Church, Henry C. Murphy, John T. Hoffman, John A. Dix, Henry W. Slocum, Wm. F. Allen, and William Kelly. But one object appeared to animate the entire assemblage, which was one of the largest that was ever drawn together by a State Convention, and that was to bring out the strongest man. The Conservative Republicans, in many instances, pressed the name of General Dix, but soon wheeled into line for Hoffman; and after two days' canvassing the merits of the several candidates, their strength and their capabilities, it was generally conceded that Hoffman's nomination was the best that could be made. On the second day of the proceedings, Hon. A. Oakey Hall presented Mr. Hoffman's name to the Convention in a neat and appropriate speech. This was followed by Edwards Pierrepont, who, in seconding the nomination, announced that he had been requested by General Dix to withdraw his name, and to announce that he (Dix) was in favor of John T. Hoffman.

Other speeches were made, eulogistic of Mr. Hoffman, by Francis Kernan, of Utica; Darius A. Ogden, of Yates; and Abraham Wakeman, of New York, when Mr. Hoffman was nominated by acclamation amidst unbounded enthusiasm.

After making the other nominations the Convention adjourned until afternoon, at which time Mr. Hoffman, having been telegraphed for, appeared and made the following address, accepting the nomination :—

GENTLEMEN OF THE CONVENTION AND FELLOW-CITIZENS: I should be less than a man if I did not admit that I am proud at this greeting. I have just entered the city of Albany. I have come here in obedience to a telegram I did not feel at liberty to disregard. During the active session of the Convention, when my name was being canvassed with others for the office of Governor of the State of New York, I did not feel at liberty to come here, because I felt that if the nomination were to be made it should be made by the delegates assembled there without any personal interference or action of my own. (Cheers.) Now that the nomination has been made, I am here to accept it in person, and thank you for the honor you have done me. (Cheers.) I appreciate, gentlemen, the honor you have conferred on me, and I also appreciate the responsibilities, the cares, the anxieties that will follow upon it ; for no man, I care not how young or how old, how vigorous or how feeble, can enter on the combat, such as we have to fight, without feeling, in the very depths of his heart, the importance of his position and of the canvass in which we are to be engaged. I feel this the more because I know there have been in this Convention many to whom I was personally a stranger, my lot in public life having been thrown in the great city of New York, and my public career having been to a great extent confined there. I feel I am under a debt of double obligation to the gentlemen from different parts of the State comprising the Convention who have chosen me as the standard-bearer of the great constitutional party. (Cheers.) I have nothing to commend myself to them but my record, such as it was. (Cheers.) During the great war through which this country has passed it was my privilege to be in position in New York, where I endeavored to oppose secession and defend the Union, and to aid in the promotion of volunteering, and I labored, at the same time, that the right of every citizen under the Constitution and the laws should be protected and held inviolate. (Cheers.) In the court of which I had the honor to be a member, while I undertook judicially to impress on all people obedience to all law, and to see that every man, so far as I had power, be protected in his constitutional and legal rights, I did not hesitate to visit the penalties of the law on those who violated the law. (Cheers.) I have endeavored, in the position in which I have been placed, to stand in opposition to centralization of power in the State and elsewhere. I was opposed to the "farming out" of the city of New

York to partisan legislatures, and I stand opposed to it to-day. (Immense cheering.) When the war was at an end, with my fellow-citizens I declared that the war having ended, peace should come. At the New England dinner, December, 1865, when a distinguished United States Senator said that according to the old Puritan doctrine it would be necessary to shed more blood for the remission of sins, I took my stand and said : " Blood enough has been shed to remit the sins of the universe." I declared then, and on the 8th of January following, that we were on the eve of great and important events, and that for the time all political antagonism should be buried. There I took my stand, and avowed my readiness to unite with all men, whoever might be the leaders, under the battle cry of "The Union and the Constitution ; " to sustain the President (cheers) in his determination to restore every State to its proper position in the Union. (Cheers.) My fellow-citizens, pardon what, perhaps, may seem to be the egotism of these remarks ; but it is due to those I have never had the pleasure to meet before, to tell them what has been my platform, and is at present. I feel as I stand here, in the presence of this Convention, and selected as I have been by the great constitutional Union party, that I have been honored among men who have been honored everywhere. I have been mentioned in connection with Dix, Murphy, and Slocum, and other distinguished names ; I have been chosen by the unanimous voice the standard-bearer of this great Conservative Union party of the State ; and when I feel that the selection has been made from among names honored everywhere, wherever mentioned ; that I have been in this Convention named in association with Dix, Murphy, Slocum, Kernan, and that among them all you have done me the distinguished honor of saying, that in view of the present condition of affairs, in view of the emergencies of the day, I am the man to run this fall for the office of Governor of the State of New York, I feel it due to you and due to myself to state every doctrine I have advocated. I cannot make any long speech. I stand here a constitutional Union man, pledged to carry out what the Senate of the United States promised in its resolutions, referred to in your second resolution, and what General Grant promised when General Lee surrendered to him. (Cheers.) What is the issue ? It is, whether the war for the Union shall be followed by a Union ; it is whether, secession having been put down, in theory and practice—whether, slavery having been abolished—whether, the South having submitted to the authority of the Government, the Southern States shall be represented in the Congress of the United States by loyal men. That is the question of the day. The Radicals themselves differ in some of their propositions. Mr. Thaddeus Stevens, on one hand, declares for universal confiscation, and universal suffrage, and universal ruin. Mr. Horace Greeley, representing another element, on the other part, declares for universal suffrage and universal amnesty. Others are for this plan, others for that. But the great practical question is what I have just stated: whether the States now kept out of the Union shall be represented in the Congress of the United States by loyal men. (Great cheering.) That question will be determined this fall. A distinguished Radical politician, travelling in the cars to-day, admitted that in his judgment the contest would be a close one. (Cheers.) Perhaps it will, gentlemen—that depends upon you. It depends upon you whether, when you leave this hall and return to your homes, you organize the State for the purpose of victory. If that be done, this great question, on which we have started, will be decided with triumph. Gentlemen, the Radical power and party in this country are a power and party for destruction—it can tear down, but it can never build up. (Cheers.) There is a spirit of intolerance about it that can crush, but can never restore. It assails every individual right, it attacks every local organization which is antagonistic to its own interests, and seeks to centralize within itself that power which would enable it to perpetuate its baleful influence on you forever. They talk of victory. Where is the accession to their strength? From whence does it come? I can form no idea, unless they hope, by a shameless open bid they have made for the votes of Irishmen, that they can catch them by the spurious pretexts they set forth. I am told that they anticipate entrapping a few men who have heretofore voted with the Democratic party, and that they will now be with them. Why, I tell them that the men there and elsewhere will perceive too readily that the policy they are advocating towards the Southern States is the same policy which England has enforced against Ireland (cheers), and they will be ready to strike a balance between profession on the one side and practice on the other. They will be ready to see that the same spirit of intolerance which keeps the States out of the Union, which declares who are fit and who are not fit to be trusted with political priveleges—that same spirit of intolerance which interferes with social relations here and elsewhere, will, when the present hobbies are worn out, assail not only the suffrages, but the religion of the men whose support they are now courting. (Cheers.) Now, my fellow-citizens, I have about done. These are desultory remarks. No man who appreciates the magnitude of the great State of New York—its interests, its wealth, its power, present and prospective, and who knows that by a convention of the great conservative men within it he has been chosen for the time being as their leader, can help feeling the importance and solemnity of the occasion. These remarks are not made, therefore, in a spirit of excitement. We go forward from this day in the battle throughout the State; we fight the men who advocate centralization of power, the men who call themselves "loyal." Against the great body of the supporters of these Radical leaders we have not a word to say; but when these Radicals assume all the loyalty of the land, I ask them, "What do they mean? Loyalty to what? Loyalty to the Constitution?" No. They deny its application to the whole Union, and tamper with it, while States are unrepresented. Loyal to the President? No, they vilify him. Their test of loyalty consists in submission to the action of a majority in Congress. (Cheers.) Has the test of loyalty come to this? Has it come to this in free and independent America? No man can be loyal who does not give his willing assent to the action of a majority in Congress. You and I have been taught in the days of old that it was love of country, love of union, obedience to the Union, that constituted loyalty; that it was that that determined whether a man was loyal or not. But, thank God! none of us have been brought up in a school in which we were taught to say that a determination to keep ten States out of a representation in Congress was the test of loyalty in Americans. (Cheers.) Am I right? ("Yes.") Then, fellow-citizens, enter on the contest which we have commenced with zeal and determination. Recollect the issue! It is the rights of the people; it is the rights of the States as well as the United States; it is the preservation of the Union of States. You have in this contest shown your appreciation of the Union of States, the rights of States, and of the interests of the States, in opposition to those who are working for the disunion of the States and the disruption of our national unity. In their State Convention at Syracuse last week they forgot the State of New York, and in their resolutions and platform they have made no reference to it. Is that because the policy of the Radicals either in its legislative or executive departments is so defined and is so popular that no further declaration of principles is needed? If so, I have yet to learn it. They have ignored the great is-sues which are vital to the State of New York, and have adopted a national pol-icy which keeps States disunited and delays indefinitely the restoration of the Union. Against such a policy the conservative men of the great State of New York will contend, with an assurance of triumph. Long Island and Manhattan will thunder forth majorities in favor of the principles declared at this Conven-tion, and if you meet them with your usual vote, your success is certain. In the canvass in which you are engaged, I will, so far as health permits, discuss those public questions in a more satisfactory manner than now. (Great cheers.) I know the contest will be an angry and bitter one. In its bitterness I will take no part. If this canvass cannot be conducted by me as a patriot and citizen ought to conduct it, I would rather not conduct it at all. (Cheers.) I stand by the record of my life. There is no public or private act of mine that fears in-vestigation. (Cheers.) If there is to be vituperation and abuse in this contest —and they threaten to resort to it—I shall not follow them. Our policy is not to be on the defensive, but on the offensive. (Cheers.) There is now a disposition to yield past differences, and men of different shades of political opinion are uniting for the common good. (Cheers.) As the President said to me the other day in the streets of New York, when he was surrounded by thousands, "The country can yet be saved." (Cheers.) Starting on that the-ory, to save the State and save the country, to make the entering wedge by which the hosts of Radicalism can be routed, is to be the thing we are to ac-complish. We are to take them in their citadel. The war is to be offensive on our part. They must defend themselves. We are now right upon the record.

The campaign at once commenced in earnest. The Republican papers were not slow to commence their abuse of Mr. Hoffman, but their slanders were easily and effectually silenced by the letter of lead-ing New York Republicans, nominating Mr. Hoffman for Recorder a second term, and paying a high tribute to his ability, judgment, and patriotism. This and other avowed evidences of the esteem in which Mr. Hoffman was held by leading Republicans while acting as Recorder, had the effect to check much of the partisan abuse that would otherwise have characterized the campaign of that year.

Mr. Hoffman opened the campaign personally in Elmira, on the night of September 25. The meeting was one of the largest that ever convened in the western part of this State. His address there being the key-note of the campaign, we present it entire. Its pertinency and strength have a decided bearing upon the present canvass:—

SPEECH OF JOHN T. HOFFMAN.

LADIES AND GENTLEMEN:—I came into your beautiful town this morning, the candidate of the young men for the Governor of your State, a stranger personally almost to every man within the limits of your city. But I have had a greeting and welcome accorded so sincere, so enthusiastic, that I feel truly grateful to you all. (Cheers.) I stand before you to-night the representative of great prin-ciples, and of a great conservative party, made up of men who for some time past have not acted in political association. For the time has come—the neces-sities of the age demanded that it should come—that for the great end of securing a speedy restoration of all the States to their rights as States under the Constitution, men should lay aside past prejudices, past antagonisms, and meet together in one common body for one common end, the good of the whole United States of America. (Loud cheers.) I do not stand here to-night, ladies and gentlemen, to say one single word in regard to the candidate for Governor of the State of New York. I leave it to my enemies to abuse me; I leave it to the record of my life to defend me. (Cheers.) I announced at the beginning of this campaign that I should indulge in no personalities; and I declared then, as I declare now, that if the record of a life in the leading city of this great country will not justify me before the people of the State, nothing that I can say in my own behalf, and in my own defence, can secure to me their approval and their suffrage. I have no charges to make against my opponents; I have nothing to say as to them personally. The assault I have to make to-night is upon their policy and their principles, and I shall do that to the best of my ability, sparing nothing in the attack. Now, my fellow-citizens, let us look for a moment at the great issue of the day. I can hardly hope to add anything to the forcible speech of the distinguished gentleman who presides at this meeting. I do not hesitate to say that I have not heard in this campaign, nor have I read so much said in so few words which must commend itself to the good judgment of every patriotic American citizen. (Cheers.) Nevertheless, in my own way of presenting this question, I shall proceed to do it with such brevity as is consistent with the occasion. This country has just passed through a terrible struggle, a war which has convulsed it from one extreme to the other. It never could have passed successfully through it if the hearts of the great mass of the American people, representing all parties, had not been in the contest. We will not look at the past. We will not dwell upon the assaults which have been made upon individual men and individual parties. The great truth stands out, prominent and beyond dispute, that the whole people of the North, almost *en masse*, have united their energies, their talents, and their capital, in the one great work of preserving the union of the States, for which their fathers fought and bled; and however they may have differed as to the means and peculiar manner in which the war should be conducted, they were agreed upon the one great point, that it should be so conducted that all the States of all this Union should be kept within the Union, under the Constitution, and under the restrictions imposed thereby. For that end, how many hundreds of thousands of lives have been sacrificed, how many thousands of millions of dollars have been expended, how many houses have been desolated, how many young hopes have been blighted, how many old heads have been bowed down in sorrow and brought to the grave, for that one end, the preservation of the union of these States! If, during this whole contest, one man or woman had been asked this question: "When this war is over, shall the States in rebellion be kept out of the Union?" there would have been one unanimous and emphatic "No." (Cheers.) That, then, was the object for which they fought. That, then, was the object for which sacrifices of life and sacrifices of money were made; and now that the war is ended, now that the rebellion has been subdued, now that the admitted cause of the rebellion—slavery—has been abolished, and now that the South have declared that their own debt shall be repudiated, now that they have fulfilled the obligations imposed upon them by Congress when the rebellion was suppressed, we still find the great majority of that Congress, representing the Radical party in this country, declaring with one voice that the States which our people fought to keep in the Union, shall not come in. And the question which you are to determine in this election in the Empire State is, whether the North is with the Radical party upon that issue.

My friends, I have said that the rebellion has been subdued. If it has not been subdued, then the war is not yet over. But it has been subdued : the President of the United States has proclaimed peace throughout the land : every soldier in rebellion has gone to his home. There is not an armed force arrayed against the Government from one end of this country to the other. There has not been an outbreak, with one or two exceptions, in the South since Lee's surrender. There has been a riot in New Orleans, and that is all. With that single exception, history affords no parallel to the entire submission exhibited by the Southern people to the results of the war brought on by themselves and ended by the heroic valor of the people of the North. I ask the chairman of this meeting, I ask you, when the war was being waged, was it not your fear, as it was mine, that even after the war was closed the discontented spirits of the South would form guerrilla bands, and keep the country in a condition of inquietude for years to come ? Did not Mr. Lincoln himself declare that he feared, after the war was over, that Congress would have to take action to compel the Southern people to send representatives to Congress ? But what is the picture ? Entire submission to the authority of the Government ; readiness to receive propositions proposed by Congress ; slavery cheerfully and willingly abolished—the sacrifice of what to them, or many of them, was all they had ; the debt, to which many of them were pledged by every dictate of honor, repudiated ; obedience to law ; the States, many of them, passing laws to protect the rights of every citizen, white and black ; giving every evidence they can of their submission to the result of the war, and asking nothing in return but that they should have the rights that the Constitution guarantees to every State and to every citizen of every State. (Cheers.) Have I told the truth ? I know not what may have been told to the people of Elmira by this travelling company of Radicals who are circulating through the State, nor do I care ; for men who come from any section of the country begging the rest of the country to keep them out of the Union, are not worthy of the confidence of the American nation. (Cheers.) The man who claims to be a representative of a Southern State and of the Southern people, who does not want his State to have its representation under the Constitution, might far better stay at home than go travelling about the country at the expense of loyal leagues and Radical politicians and assessments upon office-holders, to denounce his own people, and beg that they may be kept out of the Union. (Cheers.) I shall not stop to ask what declarations these men have made to the citizens of Elmira ; I appeal to the history of the day, to the journals of the day, to the temper of the Southern people, to all the evidences that have been furnished to any community, if the picture I have presented of the entire submission of the Southern States to the authority of the Government is not a true picture in all its features. (Applause.) Now, if it is, what then ? If there is anything of which an American citizen feels proud, it is of his honor. If there is anything of which an American citizen feels proud, it is when he can say throughout the world, " I am an American." If there is anything of which an American could desire to boast, it would be that the American nation never breaks treaties and never violates its plighted faith. Gentlemen, to what did Congress plight the faith of the nation in reference to this war ? That it was not waged in any spirit of oppression or with any purpose of subjugation, but merely to keep the States in the Union, and when the war was closed to give them their rights under the Constitution, and the protection which the Constitution guaranteed to them. Was not that published in every paper throughout the land? Was not it announced from this platform and from every platform throughout the country? Was not it the leading cry under which men, without regard to party, rallied to our standard and to the public meetings to encourage the soldiers who had gone to the war? (Applause.) If the cry had been, "It is prosecuted to put down rebels and keep out the Southern States," would there have been the same enthusiasm? ("No, no.") But no, Congress in solemn resolutions declared the object of the war, and Congress, out of honor, in consideration of this sacred pledge, is bound to-day to admit loyal representatives of the people of the South. (Applause.) I have spoken of the pledged faith of the nation. Was there nothing else? When Lee surrendered to Grant, what did Grant tell him? "Lay down your arms, go home, and as long as you are obedient to the Constitution and the laws you shall be protected in your rights as American citizens." And is there a soldier or officer who would stand before General Grant to-day and say: "The word you pledged to them shall be broken?" ("No, no;" cheers.) When the President of the United States travels through this country with Grant on one side and Farragut on the other, they are two living witnesses of the sense of the obligation which they feel to the plighted faith of the nation. (Cheers.) General Grant may declare he is no politician, Farragut may declare he is no politician; but when these two noble heroes of the war stand side by side with the President, while the people of Indiana, it may be, refuse to hear him, you may be sure that they desire with him to secure the representation of all the States by loyal men in the Congress of the country. Let the soldiers who have returned from the battle-field, who are now at home, scattered through this country, determine for themselves, when this election comes, whether they stand with Grant and Farragut and the President, or whether they stand with Stevens and Greeley and Butler and Wendell Phillips, *et id omne genus*.

Now, my friends, we have got a little to say about Congress. I shall endeavor not to exhaust you by any long speech, for you perceive that my throat is not in the best condition. A speech in the open air, to such an audience as I have had to-day, is not calculated to improve it. But I have my duty to perform in this campaign, and I mean to perform it, let the consequences be what they may. (Cheers.) I have said Congress denies to these States representation in Congress. Now, I propose to see what Congress once insisted on in reference to this same question. In 1864, just before the adjournment of Congress, a bill was passed for the reconstruction of the States. It was introduced into the Senate, and finally passed the House on the last day of the session. It did not receive the approval of the President, for the reason, as he said, that it passed so late that he had not time to give it the examination he desired. But it embraced what Congress was willing to do. The first amendment simply referred to who might vote in the State elections, for the State conventions that were to assemble. The second and third articles were as follows:

2. Involuntary servitude is forever prohibited, and the freedom of all persons is forever guaranteed in the State.

3. No debt, State or confederate, created by or under the sanction of the usurping power, shall be recognized or paid in the State.

The bill further provided that when a constitution containing these provisions should have been framed by the convention, and adopted by popular vote, it should be recognized as the government of the State.

And then Congress declared, by every act which could make it more binding, that those amendments being adopted, the Constitution should be ratified in Congress. Mr. Lincoln, in the same message in which he gives his reasons for not signing the bill, which was that it was presented for his approval less than one hour before the *sine die* adjournment of Congress, goes on to make a proclamation, saying that the provisions therein were acceptable to him. Congress did not claim then that the Southern States should adopt amendments to the Constitution, which they now claim should be adopted; and that was at the close of the session of 1864. But Congress at the la t session passed an act making it necessary for certain other amendments to be adopted by the Southern people. They nowhere say that when those amend s nts are adopted by the Southern people they shall have representation in Con ress. On the contrary, a bill was introduced in Congress declaring that when these amendments were adopted by the States, then they should have representatives in Congress, *and that bill was defeated in the House.* I come, therefore, to the question of these constitutional amendments, because they are important amendments in this canvass. The Chairman of this meeting has said, and said very properly, that the question is not now whether constitutional amendments shall be adopted or whether they shall not be adopted. We are not called upon in this canvass to vote upon that question. He has stated very truly that the question is simply whether the Southern States shall have representation, independent of the question of the adoption of these constitutional amendments. I desire to say a single word upon the amendments themselves, on the theory that if they were adopted these States should have admission. Now, these amendments are numerous. There are four or five of them, and it is the first time, I think, in the history of the country, that any attempt has ever been made to require States to adopt a series of amendments to the Constitution at one time. One of these amendments, and a very serious amendment, which is talked about to the people a great deal by the Radical orators and speech-makers going about, is the one that declares that hereafter representation shall only be allowed to the voting population of the States; or, in other words, that wherever male persons above the age of twenty-one years are excluded, they shall not be calculated in the basis of representation. You find these men asking the people, and you find people asking you, if the Southern States only had a certain amount of representation when all the blacks were slaves, before the rebellion, why they should have any greater representation now? And it is a question which strikes men very forcibly. They say, perhaps justly—I am not disposed now to dispute the proposition— that States which have been in rebellion should not come back into the Congress of the country with greater representation than they had when they commenced. That is a practical and important question. It matters little what my views are, but I do not hesitate to say that if the amendment stood alone, and I was satisfied of the right of Congress to exact it as a condition to the admission of these States, I would give it my hearty approval. But first I deny the right of Congress to require the adoption of that or any other amendment as the condition precedent of the admission of these States to representation in Congress. They will tell you it is part and parcel of the war measures necessary to bring about perfect peace and harmony throughout the land. When the abolition of slavery was required as a condition, there was sense in that, because all men, by virtue of the force of circumstances, admitted that the institution of slavery, which had been the disturbing cause of the war, and of so many irritations, was of necessity wiped out by the war, and, therefore, as a necessary war measure for the suppression of the cause of the war, there was justice in exacting it;

and whether it was constitutional or not, the people of the South acquiesced in it. Just so in regard to the repudiation of the Southern debt—it would not do to let a people pay a debt contracted in the service of the rebellion; while every sense of prudence demanded that the country's debt should be paid, incurred in putting down that rebellion. But when these subjects were out of the way there was nothing left necessary for the peace and harmony of the country. And when Congress propose these amendments to change the representation in Congress, they do it merely to perpetuate their own political power in the body in which they are acting. (Applause—"That's so.") Is it not so? Let us see. I take it for granted that there is no one here who fears that the few members of Congress who come back from the South are going to be able to revolutionize and overthrow the Government, if they had the disposition, against the immense Northern majority against them. But the Radicals say the rebels of the South may unite with the Conservatives and keep them out of power, and so they want an amendment of the Constitution to diminish the Southern representation. See where this leads you. Is it not a startling position to be taken, that a Constitutional amendment must be adopted to keep a mere party in power? Some day New England may get so much exercised upon the tariff question, in favor of a high tariff, and the great Western States so much exercised against the high tariff, that whatever party can get a controlling majority in Congress for the time being, may take it into their heads that they will reduce the representation of the other section. New York might take it into its head, as I think it will this fall, to overthrow these Radicals (cheers and laughter) and elect a Conservative ticket, and the Radical members of Congress may suggest that its representation in Congress shall be diminished. Now, this is not absurd; I am only showing just where this argument leads you. It can lead you nowhere else, because there can be no motive for the amendment I have spoken of being insisted upon as a condition precedent, other than that of securing political and partisan power. (Applause.) Nevertheless, if it were in the power of Congress to impose this amendment, I would give it my hearty approval: I would be willing to approve it so as to remove all the difficulty in the way of the admission of the States. I have had Southern men say to me, "Sir, wrong as that amendment is, our people would adopt it to-day, if it would end this ceaseless and eternal agitation—not cheerfully, but they would adopt it. But,"—here comes the rub—"Congress never meant, when they suggested those amendments, that the people of the South should ever adopt them." I will tell you why. They added another amendment which proscribes a large class of the people of the South forever from any share in the government of the nation, or of the States. They proclaim by these amendments that no man who has taken the oath as Congressman, or judge, or member of a State Legislature, shall ever again hold a seat in Congress, although he may have been a member of the Legislature of a Southern State twenty years ago. It is very well to say that men who have been in rebellion shall not have seats in Congress, but it is not very well to say that any people shall be asked to proscribe, by their own act, the men with whom they have been in intimate association all their lives. It is not all very well to say that a family shall be called upon to proscribe its head in order to secure the right of representation in Congress, or that a father shall proscribe his son. It is not very well to claim that this country will ever have peace and harmony as long as there are a large number of men in the Southern States proscribed from all participation in the government and its affairs. And this Radical Congress knew as well as you know, that there is no people on the face of the earth who would ever consent to a constitutional amendment which would proscribe their own brothers, fathers, and friends—the men with whom they had labored and suffered. But the Radicals, knowing this, intended to go into this canvass and represent the people of the South as refusing to adopt reasonable amendments to the Constitution, and so tide over this election and the next Presidental election, and thus secure to themselves another lease of power. ("They can't do it.") If there are any soldiers here, or any sailors here, or in this town, who would see this question discussed in language so clear, so beautiful, and so expressive that it makes you feel how language is capable of expressing in the simplest way the most powerful arguments, let him read the address of the Soldiers and Sailors' Convention which assembled in Cleveland several days ago ; and I trust the gentlemen controlling the organization of this district will put it in circulation, and see that it is in the hands of every voter in the district. It is full of sense, it is unanswerable in argument, it is convincing and conclusive, and no man can reason against it for a moment. Now, my friends, so far we have discussed these amendments. We come to another practical subject, and that is—whether the people who are represented are sincere or not. *The Radical members, claiming to represent the people of the North, when they say that all that keeps the South out is their refusal to adopt these amendments, are not sincere.* The best evidence I can give upon that, in the first place, is a fact as stated in the New York *Times.* I will read the paragraph. It says: "There is not the slightest difference of opinion, so far as we are aware, in the Union party, and very little anywhere else, as to the wisdom of ratifying the constitutional amendment proposed by Congress." Well, my friend Raymond had some doubts about it when he wrote the Philadelphia address and read it ; but the circulation of his paper has been impeded among the Radicals who did not like his doctrines, and so he has concluded to administer a few doses of Radical medicine. (Laughter.) He continues: "It received every Union vote in the House, and is sustained by every Union journal throughout the country. The only point upon which differences do prevail, is as to the policy of making its adoption a condition precedent to the admission of representatives from Southern States. Upon this Union members of Congress were not agreed among themselves. Some were opposed to admitting them until after the amendment should have become part of the fundamental law, by the ratification of three-fourths of all the States. Others, like Mr. Bingham of Ohio, insisted that whenever any Southern State should ratify the amendment, that State should thereupon be admitted to representation. Others, like Mr. Boutwell of Massachusetts, and Mr. Kelley of Pennsylvania, refused to pledge Congress to admit them even after the amendment should be adopted, and others still did not deem it within the constitutional power of Congress to impose its adoption as a condition of admission to the fundamental right of representation. In point of fact, the adoption or rejection of the amendment has nothing whatever to do, as the law now stands, with the admission or rejection of members from the Southern States. A bill providing for their admission on condition of its adoption was rejected by the House, and even if every Southern State should ratify the amendment to-morrow, Congress has not pledged itself in any way thereupon to admit their representatives to Congress."

Now I ask, with what fairness and candor can men who represent the Radical party come before an intelligent audience and say that the only reason the Southern States are kept out of the Union is because of their refusal to adopt these amendments? But there is even a later evidence on that subject. The New

York *Independent*, which is one of the leading journals of the Radicals in the State—I believe it does not publish Mr. Beecher's sermons any more, which may be considered another proof of its Radical sentiment—says: "No leading Republican in Congress means to admit the ten waiting States simply on the adoption of the constitutional amendment." Mark that. It further says: "These States are to be admitted on no conditions short of the equal political rights of their loyal citizens, without distinction of race. A reconstruction of the Union on any other basis would be a national dishonor. *Until the rebel States can come back on this basis, they shall not come back at all.*"

In plain language, until the right of suffrage shall be given to four millions of uneducated negroes just freed from the bonds of slavery, not one out of one thousand of whom can read or write,—until that has been done, the Southern States shall not be again admitted into the Union. Now if there are any conservative Republicans here, and I trust there are, I do not ask them to read the *Times* to-morrow to see whether Mr. Raymond has changed his mind again ; I do not ask him to read the *Herald*—(hisses)—to-morrow, to see whether Mr. Bennett believes that the country is radical ; but I ask him to determine whether he is willing to plant himself on that platform that there shall be no union of the States until four millions of uneducated negroes shall be admitted to the suffrage ? These issues are getting plainer every day. I ask this of every man here. I ask it of every lady here—for the influence of women in the politics of the country is of itself a power, and I am glad to-night to see in this assemblage of conservative people that they are taking an interest in this matter. Let discussions upon these subjects go forward, and let the women of the country instruct their sons that they shall never exact as a condition of the enjoyment of constitutional rights any such condition as that there shall be added to the suffrages of the nation four millions of negroes. (Applause.) Now, to show you how utterly hollow is this pretence of the Radicals that they intend to give representation to these people upon the adoption of the constitutional amendments, and in order to show you the policy of hate, the policy of war, the policy of malice, the policy of insane frenzy which characterizes them, permit me to read an extract from a paper which I hold in my hand. It is an advertisement of the New York Weekly *Tribune*, published by Horace Greeley, the man who asked the President—and I will only allude to it in passing—who asked President Lincoln to submit these propositions to the country as a basis of adjustment :

"1. The Union is restored and declared perpetual.

"2. Slavery is utterly and forever abolished throughout the same.

"3. A complete amnesty for all political offences, with a restoration of all the inhabitants of each State to all the privileges of citizens of the United States.

"4. The Union to pay four hundred million dollars (400,000,000) in five per cent. United States stock to the late slave States, loyal and secession alike, to be apportioned *pro rata*, according to their slave population respectively, by the census of 1860, in compensation for the losses of their loyal citizens by the abolition of slavery. Each State to be entitled to its quota upon the ratification by its Legislature of this adjustment. The bonds to be at the absolute disposal of the Legislature aforesaid.

"5. *The said slave States to be entitled henceforth to representation in the House on the basis of their total, instead of their Federal, population ; the whole being now free.*

"6. A national convention to be assembled so soon as may be to ratify this adjustment, and make such changes in the Constitution as may be deemed advisable."

That is what Horace Greeley asked President Lincoln to agree to. Now hear what Horace Greeley says—the man who has attempted in the issues of his paper to say that he who stands before you was not true to the Constitution and Union, and charging that in 1863 I insulted the Republican party and its leaders, when he knew, and it has been published in other papers, though he would not print it, that in October of the same year his own Convention nominated me for the office of Recorder, and sent me a letter in which they said my devotion to the cause of the country had never been doubtful. Hear what he says, and I ask you when you read it to say whether such a spirit will bring peace and prosperity to the country.

"A political struggle rarely surpassed in importance or intensity has been precipitated on the country by the treachery of Andrew Johnson, and some of his official or personal adherents, to the great and patriotic party by which they were intrusted with power. The aim of this treachery is to put the steadfast loyalists of the South under the feet of the 'whipped but not subdued' rebels, and to enable the latter to glut their vengeance on the former, whom they hate and curse as responsible for the most unexpected overthrow of their darling 'confederacy.'"

In the name of Heaven, if that be true, as Horace Greeley says it is, how can he stand up in his paper and declare for universal amnesty on the basis of universal suffrage? If that be true, as he is attempting to make you believe it is, then the Southern people are not entitled to representation in Congress, or to association with patriotic men. He knows it is not true, but he circulates it to inflame the passions of the people, and mislead the conservative mind of the country. He goes on to say: "The recent wholesale massacres at Memphis and New Orleans were but conspicuous manifestations of the spirit now rampant in the South, whereof the pro-rebel triumph in Kentucky is a more recent example. The soldiers of Lee, Beauregard, Johnston, and Hood are now the dominant power from the Potomac to the Rio Grande; they elect each other to office in preference even to stay-at-home rebels; they have supplanted nearly all others as policemen of Southern cities; they are organized and officered as State militia; and they ruthlessly crush every demonstration of loyal whites or loyal blacks in the assertion of the equal rights of American freemen. The school-houses of the blacks are burned, and their white teachers subjected to violence and outrage by unhanged rebels, who relieve the work of murder and arson by cheers for Andy Johnson and execrations of Congress."

Fellow-citizens, ladies and gentlemen, mothers and fathers of children, friends of the living and the dead! is it the duty of an American citizen to give countenance to documents like that, which are circulated in every steamboat and every rail-car in the country? And to what end? "Two copies of the *Tribune* for three months one dollar." (Loud laughter.) Why, a man who would try to keep up, in this country, the spirit of hate and vengeance, a man who would try to keep up the excitement which has kept asunder the States so long, a man who would circulate broadcast through the country such matter as that, in the face of the propositions he himself had made for the settlement of the war, and do it merely for the purpose of carrying a State or a Congressional District, is not fit to live among patriots. (Applause.) Perhaps Mr. Greeley may not agree with me. If he don't, I have no doubt he will take occasion to say so. (Laughter.) I recollect once trying a man for arson, who undertook to set fire to the *Tribune* office. There was a general impression in New York that the antagonism between Mr. Greeley and myself was so great that the man would get off. But he did not. I administered the law as I thought it was my duty to do. In the midst of the riots, he had tried to burn down the office of the newspape which had done more to excite the people than any other ; but he had violated the law, and I sent him for the full term, and fined him the full fine allowed by the law. I believe that was one of the times in my life when I have been in concord with Horace Greeley. But on all political subjects I do not hesitate to express myself thus plainly. And I am willing to meet the present Executive of this State if he pleases, and so far as my strength will allow me, to discuss these questions with him before the people of the State. (Applause.) My friends, you are weary, but I am not quite through. ("Go on ; " "go on.") One would suppose that a Congress which demanded so much of the American people, could present something to their consideration which would entitle them to confidence. Through eight months that Congress was in session, and what has it done for the country ? Has it done anything towards restoring perfect peace through the land ? Has it done anything towards the diminution of taxes ? Has it done anything towards relieving the burdens which rest upon every man, rich and poor, throughout the country ? No. It has labored until the end of the session, not to reconcile the country, but to keep it divided upon this question, in order that the present election may be passed over, and, if possible, the next Presidential election, before the Southern States are allowed the right of representation. That has been the whole aim and scope of their legislation. And they ended an eight months' session, in which nothing but this had been done, by voting $50 to $100 to certain soldiers, and $2,500 to $3,000 to every Congressman. (Laughter and cheers.) And with this money to spend, as an electioneering fund, they come back to their constituents, doing what it would have been well for the country if they had done seven months sooner. And yet we are told we are to stand by Congress. It used to be, "Stand by the President." My theory always was, stand by the Government. Neither the Congress nor the Executive are the Government. Yet they say the man who stands by the President is a traitor, and the man who stands by Congress is a loyalist. Are there any such loyalists here ? Is there a man within the sound of my voice who thinks anything is to be gained by keeping States asunder ? If so, then the arguments of my friend who presides have fallen in vain, and the only hope I have for such, as some of these political preachers say, is through the power of prayer. (Laughter.) The legislation of these Radicals is characterized by a spirit of intolerance. It is so in the national Congress, and so in the State Legislature. Wherever by the proposition of constitutional amendments, or by the passage of a legislative act, they can crush out opposition majorities, there they propose the amendment or pass the act. They have tried it in the city of New York, where we can roll up at any time an immense Conservative majority (cheers), and they do it upon the theory, as they say, that there are a large number of people in the city of New York who are not fit to vote. "Universal suffrage for black men out of the State, and restricted suffrage for white men in it ! (Laughter and cheers.) Pile up your negro votes in South Carolina ; put down your Democratic Conservative vote in New York. We will do the one by constitutional amendment, and one by act of Legislature." (Cheers.) And so they pass a Registry Law for the State of New York, by which inspectors are appointed by a partisan Board of Police Commissioners, and they send the inspectors from one district to another; the native citizen is registered on swearing in his vote, but the adopted citizen, whether he be German, or French, or Spanish, or Irish, or whatever he may be, must present his naturalization papers, and if they require him, in addition to that, he must give evidence that he is the man named in them. Why, as my friend Mr. Kernan of Utica said at Albany the other day, in view of such legislation, they will have a royal time in catching the votes of the adopted citizens of the Empire State. (Laughter and cheers.)

Now, my friends, I have about done. I have said nothing about past politics and past associations. Every man in the State who is called upon to vote for me knows that I have belonged to the Democratic party always. If that is a reason why a conservative Republican cannot give me his suffrage, he and I need not talk about it. I don't deny the fact. I affirm it, and am happy to do so. But if any one can say that by a single act or declaration of mine, in the struggle through which this country has passed, I have failed in my devotion to the Union and Constitution, and can furnish evidence enough to be submitted to a packed grand jury, I will be prepared to answer. Until he can, I stand upon my record. (Cheers.) I have no act of my public or private life which fears investigation, and I fear not to go before the people of my State and advocate the policy of which I am to-day the representative. (Cheers.) The conservative people of the State of New York have united now in one great effort to put down Radicalism in the State and nation. They fight the battle in the limits of their own State. They do not look to Maine or Vermont, for the result in neither of those States dictates the course of the Empire State. (Cheers.) Let the tide of Radicalism surge, fostered by Radical legislation ; New York votes for itself, and has not yet reached the point where she allows the elections of Maine or Vermont to influence her. What may be the result in Pennsylvania I do not say, I do not care. I hope and trust and believe that it will be carried by the conservative men of the State, but if the great influences fostered there by Radical legislation, and the great power of office-holders there yet in the confidence of Radical men, shall still prevent that State from acting in the ranks of this great conservative movement, New York will fight the battle herself, and establish herself a perfect bulwark against the surging tides, come they from whence they may. (Cheers.) I stand as the representative of this party to-day, chosen without my agency, chosen because the Convention believed I was the candidate to be presented to the people—a compliment and honor which I have not deserved and which I appreciate ; mentioned as I have been with the gallant Dix and the other men named in that Convention ; and I am proud to know that, foremost among my friends to-day, ready to work and labor for me in this canvass, is that man whose name I have just mentioned—John A. Dix. (Cheers.) I trust that after this election we shall be able to devote ourselves to something besides the discussion of this great question of national policy. I trust that measures may be taken to prevent the wasteful extravagance in the expenditure of the public money, to develop the resources of this State in every possible way under the constitution of the State, to foster canal enterprises and railroad enterprises wherever by being fostered they may add to the material wealth of the State, and thus we shall be the more entitled to our motto of " Excelsior." Let us devoutly look for this end, and earnestly pray and labor for it. As I came up this morning in the train, passing through the beautiful valley in which it runs, it seemed to me as if it was one of the most beautiful mornings my eyes ever beheld. The early morning mists were rising from the valley, creeping up the mountain side, and disappearing over the mountain top ; and I could not but indulge a silent prayer that the mists of prejudice, hate, fanaticism, and passion which threaten to overwhelm the land, might disappear as they disappeared, and vanish in the clouds. (Applause.) And as I rode along I saw the doors of the laborers in the farm-houses standing open ; I saw the smoke from the early fire curling up into the morning. I saw the cattle feeding, as it were, upon the thousand hills. I saw the little ones playing around the doors of the houses while the father went forth to his labor. I saw around me peace, plenty, happiness, greatness, and power. I said to myself, This land has passed through a struggle, but this State, with all it has suffered, does not to-day know what war is. Then I thought of the ravaged and desolated plains of the South, the terrible judgments visited on them for their rebellion on the Constitution of the United States—judgments which they admit they deserve—judgments which Heaven sent upon them; I thought of States so poor that they could hardly carry on their own local governments; with a people so poor that they could not hardly furnish the necessities of life; with households so desolate that there was hardly one in which a father or son or brother had not been taken away. I thought of their utter submission to the Constitution of the country and the results of the war. I saw them standing there, pleading with Northern men, now that the war is over, to let peace and good-will return to the country. I saw them with outstretched arms, saying, "Men of the North, we have violated the Constitution and laws; we have suffered the consequences; we are willing to abide by the results, and in the name of Heaven stretch out your hands to us; let the spirit of fanaticism, hate, and prejudice die out, and let peace and good-will reign throughout the land again." And as I thought of this I felt that I could go among the people of my State with renewed heart and renewed courage in this cause, confident that the conservative men, without regard to past prejudices, will earnestly unite in this work of restoration and regeneration. (Loud cheering.)

Mr. Hoffman spoke in Rochester, September 27th, in Buffalo, September 29th, and in Brooklyn, October 5th. All these addresses were profoundly logical, terse, and vigorous in their discussion of the great issues of the day. Mr. Hoffman grasped the situation as with a master mind, and, in his arraignment of the partisan Congress, dealt the Radicals more severe blows than they received from any other source during the campaign.

On the 10th of October Mr. Hoffman delivered a cogent and masterly speech before one of the largest and most enthusiastic political assemblages that ever convened in Syracuse. The following are his closing sentences, embodying points upon taxation, and the spirit of intolerance displayed by the fanatics toward our adopted citizens:

And now, my friends, enough of this dry argument. I do not stand before the people of any State to excite their prejudices. I do not want to excite their passions. This is a time above all others for a serious consideration of the questions of the day. The interests of the country demand peace. We have had war enough. It has resulted for the glory of the country, because it has put down the greatest rebellion that the world has ever known. We thank God for all His mercies; but now we ask for peace. And why do the interests of the country demand peace? We have an enormous debt, for the payment of which every hour's labor and every acre of land is mortgaged; and the debt will be paid. But the land and the labor is mortgaged. My friends, the farmers who may have had mortgages upon their land when the war commenced, and cleared it by reason of high prices during the war, must not lose sight of the fact that a mortgage has in effect been given for every acre in the country, and upon the very strong right arm of labor itself. (Applause.) Now, if a farmer mortgages his farm for the sake of keeping it, he does wisely. But after he has covered his farm all over with mortgages, and has got half improved and the other half fenced, if unimproved, occupied by a discontented tenantry, who take no interest in the enlargement or cultivation of the farm because they have been excluded from a voice in what shall be done, he might better have never borrowed money upon mortgage. The best thing he can do is to tear down the middle fence which divides the party, and say to the men who occupy it: "Go to work and develop the farm, and we will meet together in the evening and talk about the management of this land. Develop your resources, sow your seed, put yourselves in condition to pay this mortgage off; I want to do your pleasure." Now that is just exactly the position of the people of the North. We *can* pay it; if necessary we *will* pay it: but there is no earthly reason why these men of the South who have made us incur the debt should be kept from developing the resources, so that they can do nothing toward paying the principal or the interest of the obligation. This is not a question in which only the South are interested. The great North is interested too. (Cheers.) It appeals to them. There is no reason why you should pay two dollars of the debt while the man south of Mason and Dixon's line will pay but one of it. What proportion of the income tax do the Southern States pay? It amounts to nothing. They have levied a special tax upon cotton, but who pays it? *You who buy it.* What have the Southern people done toward it? (A voice—"Nothing.") Why? Because they are down. I dined the other day in New York with Governor Jenkins of Georgia. He told me that in the State of Georgia, which is the Empire State of the South, they had resources enough to contribute all their share toward the payment of this debt. "But," said he, "we cannot develop them. Everything is unsettled. We passed last winter a series of laws for the incorporation of companies to invite Northern capital down there to develop our resources." Said I, "Why didn't you send up your law here, to let the people know what you were doing?" "Sir," said he, "we did not have money enough in the State Treasury to pay for more printing than was needed in the public offices."

Now that thing would not continue if we had peace in the land, and if these men were permitted to go back into the Congress of the country, not for the sake of holding offices, but for the sake of feeling that they were again a part and parcel of the Government. You would find no trouble whatever in developing the resources of the South. You would find your taxation diminished, greenbacks nearer the value of gold, the income tax lessened, and the tax decreased on everything you eat, drink, and wear. Mr. Lincoln said, in his plain, practical way, that it was easier for all the United States to pay the debt than for half of it. And you all know that this policy of separation compels the men of the North to pay more than their proportion of the debt. Therefore it is to their interest that this principle of exclusion should cease. Are there gentlemen here owning national securities? Suppose the policy of the Radical leaders is to prevail, and you had assurance of it to-day, would you buy more? or would you sell what you have got, if you could get the present price? Let us see. General Butler, who is in the paid employ of the Central Radical Committee, delivering speeches from one end of this country to the other, the other day took open ground in favor of impeaching the President of the United States, and that it would be done at the next Congress. (Hisses.) Do you know where that would lead? I do not, and do not pretend to prophesy. But if you thought that at the next session a collision was to occur between the President and Congress by this threatened impeachment, do you think your bonds would go down or up in the market? (Voices—"Down!") Mr. Butler is not the only man who talks thus. Look at Mr. Sumner's speech made the other day in Massachusetts. Does he not talk about impeachment? He does. And upon what theory? The *madness* of the President! My friends, I do not stand here to create any false alarm among people; I do not think that is my policy or character. I give you nothing but the declarations of their leading men; and I tell you the mercantile men and the capitalists of the great financial centres are becoming alarmed at this great question. And well they may be. It is getting to be a serious matter when Congress and the leading men of it talk about impeaching the President of the United States because his policy does not agree with theirs, when his policy is founded on the Constitution of the country, and theirs only on pretended amendments to it. But I give you only the facts. I want you to imagine the consequences. Suppose, not so bad as that, that these Radical men should come into absolute power at Washington after Mr. Johnson's term is served out. Suppose that such a man as Stevens should be elected President of the United States. And suppose, though perhaps that is hardly supposable, that General Butler should be appointed Secretary of the Treasury—(contemptuous laughter)—or suppose some one like him to be, what would you give for your Government securities? (Laughter.) My friends, in all seriousness, any country on the face of the earth which has passed through four years of war, been able to maintain its credit as we have, subdued the greatest rebellion that ever existed utterly and thoroughly, so that there is not a vestige of it left in the South, can have no interest after that but peace. And the man, I care not who he is, who stands up before an audience of his countrymen and endeavors to instil into their minds any other ideas than those of forgiveness and of peace, injures his audience, injures his State, injures his country, and injures humanity everywhere. (Loud applause.)

Can it be possible that the great North, Northwest, and East are standing to-day in favor of the exclusion of States, because, as some men say, their representation under the present basis is to be a little larger than it was before? How many would it be—ten or twelve? What is the best guarantee that the people of the North—and when I speak of the North I mean the whole country except the Southern States—could have? Mr. Sumner talks about guarantees for the future. What are the best guarantees? So far as the South is concerned, the bitter experiences of the war through which they have passed; so far as we are concerned, our great and growing power and prosperity. Look at New York; look at the great West; look at the enfeebled South, prostrated and subdued; and think of the great and mighty North, East, and West wanting some *guarantee* from this broken-down people. (Applause.) Is there a man within the sound of my voice who can draw a paper constitution strong enough to guarantee peace that is not in the hearts of the people? ("No! no!") Why, you cannot draw a contract between two merchants that one or the other cannot break if he means to be dishonest. I know constitutions furnish guarantees. It is all well enough as long as people mean to abide by it; but when a man means to break his contract he will break it; and, if in civil life, takes a lawsuit or damages as the consequences. If among nations, they take their chances for the arbitrament of war. But the only way you can have a guarantee is to have it in the hearts of the people. And when a majority tries to force upon a minority something that is repugnant to their hearts, it only holds so long as power makes it.

(Applause.) As Thomas Jefferson said, the law of the majority can only be powerful so long as it is reasonable ; and the moment it ceases to regard the rights of the minority, that moment it becomes oppression. And the moment it becomes oppression, that moment it creates resistance ; and the moment it creates resistance it gives rise to combinations ; and when new combinations arise, what will grow out of it ? But there are vast changes to arise ; and, perhaps, New England sees it. Her power is a great power, and it hates to lose its hold. It controls the policy of the country. But the time will come when Central and Western interests may be diverse from it ; and then the policy which they now apply may be applied to them. It is a dangerous precedent to establish. Mr. Sumner said, in his speech the other day, that the hammer and the anvil were at work, and the Central States must back out ; that New England would be at work on one side and the Western States on the other ; and we must look out. Excuse me for translating figures ; but when Mr. Sumner uses such figures, it is just as well for a matter-of-fact man like me to interpret their meaning. (Laughter and applause.) And that is just what it means. (Renewed laughter.) " Take care, men of New York, that you don't go between the hammer and the anvil. Take care that when the blows are struck your interests are not crushed by them. Take care that the spirit of New England, which is the ruling spirit of the country to-day, and her interests, do not override your interests." Take care, I say, that henceforth you devote yourselves to the interests of peace and restoration ; and let us hope that before another election shall come around, the people of New York shall have some opportunity to give attention to the matters of State, and shall not be obliged to devote all their time to the matters of the general government. The Syracuse Convention never alluded to the State in the whole of their platform. And the New York *Evening Post*, which supports the ticket now, came out three days after the Convention in an article regretting that the Convention ignored the State altogether. States are ignored in this great national agitation. (A voice—"That's wrong.")

A few words and I am done. I would not come before an audience of my fellow-citizens anywhere and make an appeal to any particular class of them. I think it is beneath the dignity of a great party, no matter what its character ; and it is not worthy of a candidate of it to attempt to appeal directly to the passions and prejudices of any particular class in the community. I am told, however, that a distinguished speaker here last night, addressing the other side of the house, did make an appeal to a certain portion of the population of the town, in relation to the course of the Government as to the disposition of arms to Fenians ; in other words, that that gentleman attempted to inflame the passions of that part of the citizens known as the Irish race, by telling them that the Government sold them arms knowing that they were to invade Canada with them, and then took away those arms and arrested the possessors. With all deference to the distinguished gentleman who made the remark, I say it is not true. (Loud applause.) Those arms were sold, as other arms are sold, by the authorized agent of the Government, to whomsoever chose to purchase them. And the men arrested for that raid have been discharged by the courts. The policy of the Government is to give them back their arms, and they will get them. (Cheers.) I beg their pardon, if there are any Irishmen in this room, for even alluding to the subject. I should not have referred to it had I not understood that the speaker last night made that misrepresentation. This I hold to be the policy of holding one meeting after another, that a man who makes a misstatement may be corrected by somebody that comes after him.

(Laughter and cheers). Fellow-citizens. I am opposed to intolerance everywhere, and I think the spirit of intolerance which now prevails through this State and country ought to be done away. A little incident occurred in my presence in the cars on the way here to-day. Men professing the religion which we all adore, were irritated and excited because the President of the United States had yesterday a proclamation issued calling upon the people to render thanks to God for all His mercies, on the 29th day of November. One asked what business he had to fix a day for thanksgiving. That is an illustration of the spirit of intolerance which should be put down. I care not where it is to be found, whether in the halls of Congress or the State Legislature. It behooves you, ladies and gentlemen, in every department and station of life, to try and calm the passions of men. There is no hope except in the direction of peace. There its interests lie. If there is much to forgive, so much the better for those who extend forgiveness. And let men, from day to day, in the churches and the houses throughout the land, offer up the prayer which we have learned from infancy, to forgive as they hope to be forgiven. Let them remember all those sacred words, and that the rule is to be applied not only by individual to individual, but by class to class, by section to section, by State to State, and by a great government to the whole people—(cheers)—and that it remains now to be seen whether, this war being over, the American people can be as magnanimous and just in time of peace as they have been brave, self-sacrificing, and enduring in time of war. (Great applause.) In the firm belief that the action of the people of this city in the coming election will vindicate this doctrine, I leave you now. I thank you, my friends, for the attention you have given me, and I trust there is no one within the limits of this town who will be offended at anything I have had to say, and that I shall leave it with at least as many friends as I had when I came here. (A voice—" You will, and more too.") Whether I do or not, I shall know by the returns which we get from this town after the election on the 6th of November. (Laughter, and enthusiastic applause.)

On the 23d of October, Mr. Hoffman addressed the citizens of Binghamton, in a speech marked by its dignity of tone, logical conclusions, and calm yet effective oratory. He continued his searching arraignment of Congress for adopting a policy of proscription, and initiating a reign of hate and discord throughout the Union, and reiterated, in firm but respectful language, his belief that the policy of the Radical leaders, in and out of Congress, was calculated to engender and continue the bitterest strifes and animosities among the people of both sections.

SYMPATHY WITH IRELAND.

Pausing amid the labors of the heated political canvass, Mr. Hoffman, on the 26th of October, 1866, addressed a letter to President Johnson, upon the subject of the arrest and confinement of Fenians in Canada. The Board of Aldermen of New York had adopted a series of resolutions calling upon the President to interfere in the case of Robert Lynch, who had been arrested during the recent Fenian movement, convicted, and sentenced to death. Mayor

Hoffman emphasized the work of the Board in the following letter to the President:—

MAYOR'S OFFICE, NEW YORK, Oct. 26, 1866.

To His Excellency the President of the United States.

SIR: I have the honor to enclose herewith a copy of a preamble and accompanying resolutions this day adopted by the Common Council of this city, and approved by me, asking the interference of the Government of the United States to secure the pardon and release of Robert Bloss Lynch and other Fenian prisoners now confined in Canadian prisons. I have no doubt but the preamble and resolutions express the earnest convictions and wishes of the great majority of the people of this city, and it seems so clear to me that the pardon and release of these prisoners is alike demanded by humanity and great international interests, that I feel bound respectfully, but most urgently, to ask you to bring to bear all the influence of your administration to secure that end. I cannot doubt but such a course will bring about results most beneficial in their character and consequences.

(Signed)　　　　JOHN T. HOFFMAN, *Mayor.*

On the evening of October 30, Mr. Hoffman attended and addressed a meeting of 100,000 persons in the Cooper Institute. It was one of the largest and most enthusiastic assemblages of the campaign, made up as it was of the intelligence, the intellect, and good sense of New York's immense population. We take from this speech of Mr. Hoffman the following extract, alluding to Republican assaults made despite the public endorsement of him by leaders of the party when he ran for the second term as Recorder; and also embodying his views upon the commissions which were foisted upon the metropolis by the Radical Legislature:

A few more words upon the subject. Certain papers—partisan and venal, I will not tell which is which—in this canvass, although I opened it by declaring that I would not indulge in personalities, but would discuss measures and not men—certain papers have charged upon me various things to which I will not now particularly call your attention. But I ask you, I ask them, if they have ever yet been able to point to a single act of my official life which the people of New York would desire to rebuke? (Cries of "No," "No.") If they cannot, or if they will not, then I come to the plain question I have to ask, as following upon these preliminary remarks. If there is nothing in my official life, as Recorder or as Mayor of the City of New York, which these men can put their fingers upon as deserving of censure, then I ask the people of New York, without regard to party—the men who have visited me in my office, and in my house; who have met me in the street, and applauded what they called my firmness in the discharge of my official duties—if they will not now rise above party considerations and party purposes, and declare their unqualified condemnation of the assaults made upon him who now addresses you. (Applause.) If there has been a scheme which has originated in the city of New York, which has been at war with the best interests

4

of the people, and it has not met my opposition, let them point it out. But I call upon the merchants and owners of real estate, upon the mass of the tax-payers in this city, who have given me credit for what I have done, now in this campaign, when votes are to be cast for a Governor of the State of New York, to say whether they were earnest in their approval, or whether they now prefer party to principle, and are ready to censure a man whom hitherto they have approved.

It has been said in my hearing, and by some of my first friends, personally, in the city of New York, that I have been opposed to many things which have originated in the Legislature of the State, and which they thought calculated to promote the interests of the great city in which they live. It has been said that I have been opposed to the commissions which exist here. I have one word to say upon that subject, and I know it will meet with your approval. Am I opposed to the Central Park Commission ? No ! It is a commission of men who are not partisans. It is a commission made up of men without respect to party ; who serve the city for the sake of the city, and receive no fee or reward for the services which they render. (Applause.) And as an individual, and as an official, they have always had my earnest, cordial, and hearty support. Am I opposed to that honorable commission which has charge of the charities of the city of New York ? No. It is a commission which discharges its duties without partisan consideration or feeling. The administration of the great charities of this city was for the purpose of accomplishing the greatest good for the greatest number. A Republican Comptroller appointed four Commissioners of Charities, two of whom were Democrats and two were Republicans. A Democratic Comptroller followed his example, and appointed a Commission, two of whom were Democrats and two were Republicans. No man opposes such a commission as that. Am I opposed to it ? No. Am I opposed to the Police Commission ? I will tell you what I am opposed to. When my friend upon the right here, Governor Seymour—(great applause)—filled that Commission, he named two Republicans and two Democrats, upon the plighted faith of all men about him in public office, that they should so be continued until the end of time. When the present Governor of the State came to make his appointments, and the term of a Democratic member of that Commission expired, he appointed a partisan to fill the office, and the Police Commission became a partisan commission from that day. I honor the brave men who make up the force. They know, as I know, that for five years, in the office of Recorder, I stood by them at all hazards and under all circumstances. I believe the Governor of the State of New York has violated the faith which had been plighted when he changed a non-partisan commission into a partisan commission. (Applause.) Am I opposed to the Board of Health ? I will not disguise it ; I will admit that it has done great good in this city. But I tell you what I am opposed to, and what I was opposed to when the Board was created. I was opposed to any legislation creating any commission with great powers like that, and saying that the Mayor of the greatest city upon the American continent should not be a member of it. I am opposed to any legislation undertaking to say that in the great city of New York the chosen head of it—chosen by the popular vote—shall not be connected with any other commissions that are engaged in managing the great interests of the metropolis. (Applause.) And I tell you, when men prate about commissions, and their great intentions to do good, search it to the bottom and you will find it is a desire to seize political power for party purposes, under the pretence of advancing the interests of the people of New York. (Applause.) Am

I opposed to a paid Fire Department? I will tell you what I am opposed to. All honor to the Fire Department, whether it be volunteer or paid. But I am opposed to a paid fire department the heads of which are made up of political partisans—(applause)—who hold their caucuses in engine-rooms while buildings are burning, and while hard-working firemen are trying to extinguish them. (Applause.) And I appeal to the insurance men of the City of New York; to the underwriters; to the men whose property has been destroyed, whether that is the kind of fire department they want to continue in the city in which they live. (Voices—"No, no.") We know that the men who make it up are brave and gallant men; we know that everywhere out of the City of New York a paid fire department has been a success; but we know that in the City of New York, made up and controlled as it is of partisans, it has proved a failure, as the records of the insurance companies and property owners show. (Applause.) So much for these Commissioners. I am in favor of anything which will advance the interests of this great city. But I tell you the time has got to come, whether I occupy the chair which I now fill, or that other position in Albany, when the people of the City of New York will make up their minds that they must govern themselves. (Vehement applause.) When they will employ their energies and capacities in the selection of the best men for the public offices, and when they will rule themselves as the Constitution says they may, because it gives to the people of every county and every city the right to regulate their own affairs. (Applause.) The time has got to come when the Legislature, having given to the City of New York the worst charter that could be devised, shall cease this business of trying to patch up the evils in it by creating a lot of independent commissions, in which the Mayor, the executive officer of the city, can take no part; so that when my adversaries say to the people of New York I am opposed to commissions, I trust they understand now just what I am opposed to. I am in favor of the best government that can be devised; and the first thing I want is a charter for the city the best they can have; and the next thing I want is, that the people shall in fact govern the city as it ought to be governed.

THE ELECTION.

Thus, after a spirited and exciting canvass of about two months, during which Mr. Hoffman spoke with great effect throughout the State, the campaign was brought to a close. In all of his speeches Mr. Hoffman expressed a wish to meet his competitor, Fenton, and discuss with him the issues of the canvass; but the Republican candidate studiously ignored the request, and not until a few days before the election was his voice heard, and then in a puny speech devoid of substantial, consistent argument, and characterized by no discursive power of logic or eloquence.

The election of November 6, 1866, as we all know, resulted in the success of the Republican ticket by the insignificant majority of 13,789. It seems to be at this late day almost a work of supererogation to inquire into the causes of Mr. Hoffman's defeat. The small majority obtained by the Republicans shows that if a little more energy had been expended on the canvass by the Democracy of the interior, the result would have been different. New York city did her full duty, as she always does when the principles of constitutional government are at stake. The result of the campaign of 1866 should prove a warning to the Democracy of the State to conserve their strength and render their majorities so emphatic that neither local animosities in their own ranks nor frauds in the columns of the enemy can ever again be given as excuses for our defeat in a State election. For later revelations make it certain that John T. Hoffman was defrauded of his just returns by Republicans of the interior. But notwithstanding these frauds the result exhibited a magnificent triumph for our cause. General Slocum polled in 1865, 273,526 votes, and in 1866 John T. Hoffman polled 352,526 votes, showing an absolute gain in one year, under Hoffman's lead, of 79,328 votes; and the majority of the Republicans was reduced from 30,000 to 13,000, in round numbers.

CHAPTER VI.

EVENTS OF THE YEAR 1867.

ON the 1st of January Mayor Hoffman, as is customary, delivered his annual message to the Common Council. The document was brief, but forcible and able. The greater portion of it was devoted to a statement of the financial affairs of the city. The Mayor firmly reiterated his views upon the character of the municipal government. The various commissions which had from time to time been instituted by the Legislature had taken away nearly all the executive business of the Mayor, leaving him but little else than an empty title. He took a decided stand against the policy of parcelling the city government out in lots, and placing each under the control of a legislative commission. He believed that the people are the only proper judges of the way in which the offices of the city ought to be administered, and he regarded the old system as the safest and best.

SYMPATHY WITH THE FENIANS.

On the evening of March 13th, the Fenians of New York held an immense mass meeting in Union Square. Mayor Hoffman sent the following able and earnest letter :—

GENTLEMEN : I have this day received your letter of January 31st, inviting me to attend a meeting of the citizens of Albany, on the 5th instant, which has been called to protest against the illegal and unjust course of the British Government in its treatment of American citizens, as well as to declare their firm adherence to "those laws of our country which declare that the naturalized citizen is entitled to all the protection which the Government can afford to the native-born."

I regret exceedingly that in consequence of the pressing nature of my engagements here, and the short notice I have received of the meeting, it will be impossible for me to attend.

The subject is one in which I have long taken a deep interest, and upon which I have on more than one occasion expressed my views very decidedly.

The question, "What shall the United States Government insist upon and maintain at all hazards, in reference to the rights of our naturalized citizens abroad ?" has become to-day an all-important one, and cannot and must not be evaded or avoided. There can and must be but one answer to it, and that is, that American citizens, whether by birth or by adoption, are all free before the world—equal everywhere—owe no duty or allegiance to any government but our own, and must be guarded and protected by it.

Our adopted citizens may be counted by millions. They hold the evidence of their citizenship under the great seal of the United States of America. It is to them the nation's guarantee of protection, at home and abroad. They have on their part abjured all allegiance to foreign powers, and have taken an oath to support the Constitution of the United States. We have in return adopted them into our national family. We have conferred upon them the title of citizen, and have entered upon obligations to guarantee and defend that title against the world.

I cannot state my views upon this point more briefly and pointedly than by quoting from a communication which I had the honor to make to the Common Council of this city, on the 12th day of December, 1867, in which I said as follows : —

" The citizen adopted by us becomes bound up in our Government. In time of peace he performs all the duties which good government, law, and order require. In time of war he is, equally with all other citizens, called upon to fight for our flag, and to maintain our cause with his life if need be. We receive and enforce the duties which arise from this relation. We have simply to say, and to live up to our declarations, that we will perform our obligations, and protect our citizens against any and every power whatsoever ; to declare that citizens of the United States are free and independent. Self-preservation, as well as our dignity, our duty, and our honor require that this shall be firmly and unchangeably asserted by our Government. Suppose in the late war to maintain our national existence, in which our adopted citizens fought with such devotion and valor, Great Britain had openly taken sides against us, and had sent its soldiers to fight under the British flag, on the side of revolt, for our national destruction ; the principle contended for by England would have made every adopted citizen, born in any part of England's dominions, fighting on the side of the Union, a traitor, liable to be ignominiously executed."

Can any stronger illustration be needed to show how clearly national safety, as well as national honor, is involved in this question? We know not what the future may demand of us, so far as foreign governments are concerned, but it is not difficult to see how this question enters into our very existence as an independent nation. The recent aggressions of Great Britain against adopted citizens not guilty of any overt acts within her territory, visiting that country, had revived this question in the most striking form, and it must be finally decided. The great duty of a State is, to its citizens, to maintain their rights and to protect their persons.

I am glad to see that the people everywhere are giving expression to their views upon this subject, which affects so deeply adopted citizens of every nationality, and which belongs to the whole country. In my judgment the governments of Europe will make but feeble resistance by argument (and none at all by force) against our claims, if we make them and press them with a firmness and a dignity worthy of a great nation. Let the people see to it that their representatives do their duty.

Again expressing my regret that I cannot personally be with you, I am very respectfully yours,

JOHN T. HOFFMAN.

At the grand banquet given the following evening to John Francis Maguire upon his departure for England, Mayor Hoffman was present and made a speech, expressing his sympathy with the people of Ireland in their struggle to obtain the liberty which they had the right to exercise.

Also at the sixth anniversary banquet of the Knights of St. Patrick, on the evening of March 17th, Mr. Hoffman, in response to a toast, reiterated his well-known friendly sentiments to Ireland and the Irish people.

THE POLICE DESPOTISM.

On the 9th of May Mayor Hoffman was waited on by a delegation of German citizens, who presented a petition stating that the powers conferred on the Excise Commissioners have been greatly abused, and that the Board had adopted rules and regulations which were unjustifiable and humiliating to those who had to submit to them. They asked the municipal authorities to aid them in all legal measures they may adopt to bring about a reform of those abuses. The Mayor's response was as follows:—

MY FELLOW-CITIZENS: I am glad to see you. I am glad at all times to have any of my constituents call upon me for advice and counsel. I have listened to the statement of your complaints. I regret to say that I have no power to relieve you. The same radical and intolerant spirit in the State Legislature which has forced upon the people of this portion of the State a law which, with all its good provisions, contains many that are odious and oppressive, has deprived the Mayor of this city of the privileges and powers which of right belong to him as the chosen chief magistrate of the people. The same intolerant spirit in legislation which has conferred extraordinary power upon the Police Department, making the Police Commissioners virtually executive, legislative, and judicial officers, has made that department independent of the Mayor and all municipal authorities. The whole spirit of the Constitution of the State has been violated, and the right of the people of New York and Brooklyn to regulate their own local affairs has been taken away from them. Both cities have been placed under Commissions appointed by State authorities, and the Excise Law has been made, not for the State at large, but for a part of the Metropolitan Police District. Under that law, what is lawful *in other parts of the State*, even in *Westchester, a part of the Metropolitan District, is criminal here*. In regard to this law, which is here enforced with so much rigor and harshness, I have already expressed my opinion in a letter written some time ago. I need not repeat it. We are all of us good citizens, in favor of a judicious excise law, to be firmly administered; but we are opposed to intolerance and bigotry, in whatever form it may appear. I do not hesitate to say that, in my opinion, the Excise Commissioners are enforcing the existing law with undue harshness. They are unreasonable and unjust in their exactions. When remonstrated with by those who have no interest except to preserve popular rights and civil order, their answer is that no one directly affected by the law makes any objection. They seem by their conduct to be laboring to create excitement and provoke resistance. They make the perfect and complete submission of the people the pretext for new exactions. I am very sorry for it. I have remonstrated with one of them whom I believed to be most influential, but to no purpose. But you ask me what you shall do. I will give you the best advice I can. In the first place, you must continue to obey the law as it is, until you can modify it. Obedience to law is the first duty of the citizen. Some foolish men talk of resistance, but no sincere friend of the people will countenance that. The papers of this morning announce, by authority, it is said, of the Police Commissioners, that violence is threatened, and a riot contemplated. I hope it is not true. I believe it is not true. I most solemnly warn all people against the use of force. My views of riots and rioters are well known, and, to the extent of my power, I should deal with them in the future precisely as I have in the past. Your opponents would like nothing better than to be able to provoke you to violence. It would be *gain* to them, but ruin to you and your cause. It would change at once the current of public sympathies. Those sympathies are with you now, and are strengthening every day; disturb the peace, and you turn them against you at once. The friends of to-day would be enemies to-morrow. Thousands of good citizens who sustain you now would oppose you then. At all hazards, therefore, preserve most sacredly the peace, and frown down the first attempt to break it. Your obedience to law has won for you hosts of friends. *Be patient.* But you can with prudence and with safety *agitate.* Hold your public meetings; let your speakers be well selected, and your resolutions be well considered. Keep clear of demagogues, who will strive to use your movement for their own advancement. Look at the immense demonstrations which are being held in England, and see how rapidly they are changing the course of public events. As John Bright said at Birmingham, "Neither Lords nor Commons can resist the peaceful expression of public opinion." You can do as the people are doing there. You can, in perfect peace and order, make a series of demonstrations which will astonish the people of the State. I think we have not yet reached the point when the right of the people to assemble peaceably to discuss public questions will be denied. Let me give you another piece of advice. Let your demonstrations be on a week-day instead of Sunday, as has been contemplated. Thousands of your friends, those who condemn alike the odious features of the Excise Law and the intolerant spirit of the Commissioners, love the quiet of a Sunday, and while they concede to all men the right to spend the day according to the dictates of their own consciences, they would regret to see it disturbed by the noise and confusion of a public demonstration. What you want is to carry with you always the moral sentiment of the community. You can have it and keep it, and will be sustained by all except by those who have no idea of the liberty of others, in conscience or in conduct, beyond the liberty to think and act according to their own peculiar notions. I have spoken to you plainly and frankly. You know me, and know that I will not give you any advice which is not for your own good, and will not speak pleasant words to secure momentary applause. Do as I have told you and you will drive even the Excise and Police Commissioners to a course of moderation and fairness. If, on the other hand, you or others follow the counsels of excited or indiscreet men, you will lose everything. Be prudent and patient, and you will soon secure reasonable modification of the law, and place the power of executing it in the hands of men who can be just and firm, without being tyrannical and oppressive. The time is fast approaching when the people of New York and Brooklyn will have their rights. There is no power in the city or State which can withstand the popular will, expressed as it will be expressed. All men who think at all acknowledge that local government is better than Albany government. The experience of the past winter has taught our people that a corrupt Legislature can increase our taxes and our burdens, but can furnish no remedy for municipal or local evils. This is not a subject in which the people of New York city alone are interested. It concerns the people of the whole State. It involves the right of counties and cities and towns to regulate their own local affairs. You must organize with reference to it, and for the present make your political combinations, and regulate your political conduct, so as to secure always the election of men opposed to consolidation of power in commissions appointed at Albany. The turning-point has been reached. The next election will show the people here to be almost a unit in favor of local self-government, and against legislative oppression. They will insist that whatever excise law shall be in force shall apply to the whole State, and not to one section of it. They will rebuke that intolerant spirit which makes a rigorous excise law for New York and Brooklyn, and exempts the residue of the State almost entirely from its operation; and they will condemn that legislation which forces upon us commissions and commissioners against our will, and deprives us of the right conceded to others, of regulating our local affairs, and choosing our own local officers. I have said all that is necessary. Let your next movement be a great demonstration of fifty thousand citizens, assembled in perfect order, on some fine afternoon, speaking by its magnitude, its dignity, and its resolution, your determination to have your rights in the manner pointed out by law.

AN ELOQUENT SPEECH.

In May the great Fair in aid of the Catholic Protectorate, which is designed to rescue the Roman Catholic orphans and truants of the metropolis from a career of poverty and crime, was held at their structure on Union Square. Mayor Hoffman attended on the evening of the 20th, and delivered the following able and eloquent address:

LADIES AND GENTLEMEN: When my very excellent and much esteemed friends, Dr. Ives and Father Quinn, called upon me with a request that I would open this fair with a few remarks, I hesitated; not because I was unwilling to render service to a cause which commended itself to my judgment and my sympathy, but because I feared I could do but little to secure for it a success which I knew it deserved and desired it should meet. When, however, they told me that the ladies requested it, I felt that further hesitation would be unpardonable, because, although I am enough of a heretic to deny sometimes the authority of "the Fathers," I am too much of a gentleman to refuse to bow submissively to the will of the ladies, which, in all frankness, it is now fair to say, is on such occasions with me "Lex Suprema." The privilege and power of mingling with the people, of addressing them in their public assemblages, of uniting with them in works of charity, of encouraging them in every good deed, of cheering them in every noble-hearted effort to relieve the poor and suffering of every condition, faith, and nationality, still belongs to the Mayor of the city of New York. No legislative enactment has yet forbidden the enjoyment of the privilege, or the exercise of the power; and no commission has yet been created to monopolize the one or exhaust the other. I take this early opportunity to acknowledge the obligations I feel that so much rightful authority still remains, and I am confident that you, in the true spirit of charity, in this place dedicated to charity, will, in all charity, join with me in this acknowledgment. Do not think, my friends, that I am going to make to you a speech of uncharitable length. I have no such intention. This is the place for actual deed, not for talk; for spending money, and not for spending breath; for good deeds, and not fair speech; for actual acts, and not actual professions; for checks on banks, and not on patience; for extracts from the purse, and not from the poets; for lavishness in expenditure, and not in thought; for open hearts and hands, and not for honeyed words. And even if I desired to make an oration, how poor it would be! The cause in which you are engaged, the noble charity in which you are employed, the destitute children for whose welfare you labor, are all eloquent, and speak in a voice and with an emphasis and a beauty beside which any words of mine would be cold and formal. What is there more noble, more powerful, than the spirit of true charity? What voices can speak so musically, so pathetically, so eloquently as the voices of children pleading for aid? What ear so deaf that it cannot hear when destitute and suffering little ones call for help? What heart so cold that it cannot be warmed when good men and good women plead for those whom God in His Providence has deprived of a father's care and a mother's love?

There are thousands of these objects of charity everywhere; in the crowded tenements, in the houses of refuge, and the prisons; in the hospitals and in the streets; you meet them in the highways; you push against them at the crossings; you find them crouching at your door-step; to the right, to the left; before you, behind you, beneath your feet—everywhere; poor, naked, hungry, destitute, deserted, fatherless, motherless children stretching forth their hands and sending forth their cries to you, men and women, whom God has blessed with the choicest blessings, and supplied with wealth to be distributed among the poor and needy. It is your mission to provide for them. For them this building has been erected, and we are here to help to make it what it deserves to be and will be —a success. Many of these suffering children have been left waifs upon the great shores of society by the soldiers who fought the battles of the Union, and in whose behalf, a few years ago, the great Sanitary Fair was held, upon the very spot on which this building has been erected. The erection of the building on this street for that charity was the precedent for the erection of this. The people of this city will remember that noble work. Men and women of all stations, and nationalities, and creeds, vied with each other in making it the great event of the day. There was none so rich as to keep aloof from it ; none so poor as to refuse to contribute to its prosperity. It became a national affair because it was held in the interests of the defenders of the nation ; and statesmen and people, rich men and poor men, clergy and laity, soldiers and sailors, men, women, and children, joined hands and hearts, and made it great and glorious ; and it was great and glorious, *as this will be*, held, as it is, in the interest of their destitute children, the fathers of many of whom, Catholics as well as Protestants, languished in prisons, or lingered and perished in hospitals, or died upon the battle-field. My friends ! it is well you and all the people should understand the real character and object of this great charity in the interests of which this Fair is held. It is in aid of the " Society for the Protection of Destitute Roman Catholic Children." I am a Protestant, and devoted to my faith, and yet, recognizing one God and one Saviour of us all, I stand here to advocate this charity. It deserves the aid and encouragement and protection of all good men. This Society was incorporated by act of the Legislature of the State of New York, in April, 1863. Its beginning was feeble in money, but not in friends or prayers. Its Board of Directors consisted of twenty-six gentlemen, the Mayor, Comptroller, and Recorder of the city of New York being ex-officio members. On the 1st of May, 1863, thirteen days after its incorporation, its organization was completed. Its growth has been slow and gradual, but steady and constant. It has received, educated, and clothed more than two thousand children, the greater number having been committed to its care by the magistrates of the city and the Commissioners of Charities and Correction. In order that it may not be subjected to the charge or suspicion of attempting to proselyte Protestant children, care is taken that none but Roman Catholic children are sent to it, unless by the consent and wish of their parents or guardians. If by chance others are sent, they are immediately discharged upon the application of either parents or guardians. By private subscriptions from all classes it has received contributions of nearly $250,000, and the patronage of the city and State has been freely extended to it. The State Legislature, always largely Protestant in its organization, has made to it most liberal appropriations ; and now, by law, the *per capita* allowance to its inmates is the same as that made to other institutions organized for the care and protection of destitute children. One great and commendable feature about this institution is, that it takes these poor children out of the city and removes them to the country. It owns a farm in Westchester county. Large buildings have been erected upon it for the male children, and the noble band of Christian Brothers who have it in charge, out in the fresh, pure air of old Westchester, train these boys not only in the faith of their parents, but in the honest and earnest labor which belongs to the soil. In the language of the last annual report of the society, " Too much importance can hardly be ascribed to this feature in our system."

" Not only in this way are the children made to feel that they are contributing directly to their own support, so essential to their independence of spirit, but also, that they are thus acquiring tastes which cannot fail both to elevate their minds and strengthen their manly feelings, while they tend to wean them from those effeminate pleasures and corrupting associations so injurious to their childhood in the city, and at the same time to beget and foster in them an abiding attachment for their new country life. Evidences of this result are multiplying daily, and showing the wisdom of removing the institution from the pestiferous atmosphere of a city to the pure and invigorating atmosphere of a rural district."

On the 1st of January, 1866, there were 572 boys and girls in the institution, and nearly 500 more were admitted during the year; the average number of inmates being about 600. I have said enough to show the general character and capacity of the institution. Its character cannot be improved, but its capacity and resources can be and must be increased. There are several excellent institutions in and about the city for destitute children. All honor, I say, to the men and women of whatever creed who give their hands and their hearts to the work of carrying them on. But there is great need of more asylums, with enlarged capacities and increased facilities. The demands upon them are increasing more rapidly than their ability to meet them. The city is full of children, who will become vagabonds and criminals if not cared for. Take such children out of the streets and the haunts of vice, and place them in protectorates and asylums, and then transfer them to the workshop and the farm, and you save them from the workhouse and the prison. The real effective reforms begin with this growing generation, and genuine and wise philanthropy turns its attention eagerly to the children who are deserted and desolate. Thus briefly have I spoken of the character and objects of the charity which has called you together. One single word to those who object to the use of a portion of the public streets for the building for the fair. I agree with them, that the streets should not be obstructed by buildings of any kind. But I have alluded to the precedent established during the war, when the Sanitary Fair was held here—and it is impossible to deny to one great charity what has been granted to another. If all precedents established in the past few years do as little evil as this, we shall have occasion for gratitude. Much as I object to all obstructions in the public streets, it is better, far better, to have a temporary one like this than to have all our streets thronged with destitute children—with no roof to cover them, no hand to lead them, no protectorate to shelter them, no home to receive them, and no hope to cheer and comfort them. Better, far better to have this structure here for a few weeks, if it shall be the instrument of causing the erection of a great permanent edifice in Westchester, which shall be an asylum for houseless children for all time to come. Let all charitable people, therefore, in true charity and without bitterness, help along a good cause, and sustain the men and women who have inaugurated the movement. I know not in whose heart and head the thought of this fair originated, but it was a happy thought, and often great labor will result in great success. I have often stood upon a mighty ship; looked at it from stem to stern; studied its machinery, rising, it would seem, from its very keel away above its main decks; its timbers, bound and fastened with bolts and screws and braces; its towering masts, its humming shrouds, its flowing canvas, its wheel, its rudder, and its compass, and have thought of the vast labor and care and study expended on it, from the time the first plane was laid upon its keel until it floated on the broad ocean, freighted with human life and human hope. I stand here to-night and think of the time when the first good man thought of this "Protectorate," and began, under God, the work of forming it, and how it has grown, in all its fair proportions, into a noble structure, freighted with young life and young hopes—and I look around this fair, full as it is of Christian women and their handiwork, and think how it has grown from the small beginning of one little thought into the great and long (so to speak) triumph of many hands! I say of it as I say of all good works, God be praised, and God prosper it; and the mystery of its success, like that of all other things, becomes pleasure to me only when I recollect that "when God plants the acorn he plants with it the law of its own development."

But I am violating the pledge made at the beginning of my speech, and am detaining you too long. I know you are anxious to spend your money, and the ladies at the tables, who, like all other ladies, never talk themselves, wonder why I talk so long. I beg their pardon and yours. I beg you to go among them. You will find abundant use for your money. I am told there are many rare curiosities here, some of which will be exhibited only for a liberal fee. I will name a few at random, and ask you to look for them at every table until you find them. I will not pause to separate them into classes, for they are not classified. You will find them very much mixed. Portions of a reconstructed Union; partial views of impartial suffrage; fragments of seceded States; specimens of legislative virtue of the olden time—on exhibition, *but not for sale;* and specimens of legislative virtue of modern times—for sale as well as on exhibition (the price of which can be learned in the lobby); a section of a street cleaned according to contract; a few of the herculean efforts of the contractor to keep the city clean; a piece of Ann street as it is before it is widened, and a perspective view of it as it will be after it is widened; an article from the *New York Herald* lauding Mayor Hoffman; bottles full of the spirit of the press; and a newspaper, very rare indeed, which does not contain an account of a murder or an attack upon somebody's reputation; relics of the mayoralty power in the olden times, and a full-size portrait of the corporation when it was fed on turtle soup; chimes from the old bell-tower in the city hall, and another tower which has superseded it; an old man who was alive when the court-house was commenced, and who expects to see it finished; some money saved by the economy of legislative commissions out of the annual increase of their salaries; a few extraordinary powers which they have voluntarily relinquished; a piece of a building saved from fire under the new Fire Department, and a sample of the spirit of the old Volunteers; specie once in circulation in the country; a redeemed greenback; and the skeleton of a government contractor, who died poor during the war; ice from an iceberg; light from Luxembourg; and an animal neglected by my friend Henry Bergh, than whom no nobler-hearted gentleman lives in town. These, and thousands of other curious things too numerous to mention, you will perhaps find if you come here often, and visit all the tables and stop as long at each as it is your duty to do. Take my advice and circulate freely, not only yourselves, but your money. It will be the "medium" of many happy exchanges, not only of property, but of thoughts and pleasant memories hereafter. But better, far better than all the curiosities I have mentioned, and all the poor jokes I have perpetrated—better, far better than anything I can say—is the grand collection here of articles for sale, substantial, useful, and ornamental. Liberal givers have contributed them. Let liberal purchasers freely take them. You will get for your money all its worth, and the article you buy, and the recollection of having spent it in a good cause, will be the best dividend you could ask on your investment—a dividend payable not quarterly, or yearly, but daily, as you think of the destitution and suffering you have helped to relieve. Memories of good deeds are exceeding pleasant, and the minds of little children are as fresh and beautiful as the dewdrops in the morning. Let your united efforts rear a new building for the Protectorate. Every stone in it will be a monument of your good deeds. Recollect that the greater the capacity of institutions such as the one you seek to aid, the greater the benefit to the community in which you live. Asylums for children are better than prisons and poor-houses.

Every boy and girl taken from our streets and dens of misery, and sent to a home such as you are preparing, is one new recruit in the great industrial army, which is working and will work out the destinies of this great Republic. Two thousand abandoned children are so many aspects of evil, working mischief in ten thousand ways. The same children, cared for and protected, will in the great future exert an influence for good which cannot be estimated. I commend, therefore, the good work to your judgments and sympathies, with the fervent wish that prosperity may attend it and all who labor for it, and with the earnest hope that the few plain and simple words I have spoken may not have been uttered altogether in vain.

CHAPTER VII.

THE FALL CAMPAIGN OF 1867.

THE Democratic State Convention met in Albany, October 3, 1867, and nominated a full State ticket, with Hon. Homer A. Nelson for Secretary of State at its head. Mr. Hoffman officiated as the temporary President of the Convention, and his speech upon accepting the honor was as follows:

GENTLEMEN OF THE CONVENTION: I thank you for the distinguished honor you have conferred upon me. When I last stood in this hall it was to accept from the representatives of the people assembled here their nomination to the chief executive office of the State. (Cheers.) This greeting you have given me to-day assures me that you do not attribute it to my fault that the battle you so nobly fought was not won. (Applause.) I may be pardoned, I am sure, if I avail myself of this, my first opportunity, to thank you and the people of the State for the generous support they gave to the ticket then, and to assure you that the city of New York, which gave for that ticket nearly fifty thousand majority, and I think I may say the county of Kings, which added ten thousand more, will be ready hereafter to respond in the same thunder-tones to any ticket which you may present to them for their support, let it come from whatever direction of the State it may. (Cheers.) I shall not detain you long in what I have to say as the temporary chairman of this Convention. I shall not imitate the poetic license and the fine frenzy of the distinguished Radical Senator who presided over the Convention recently assembled in Syracuse. (Laughter.) I shall not talk to you as he did of the "Red Eye of Battle," which glared furiously at Syracuse then, and which words have become historic in connection with that subject ever since. He told those assembled there, and, through them, the people of the State, that the leaves had not fallen ten times since the banner of his party was unfurled; but he did not call attention to the fact that of American lives there had fallen ten hundred thousand since he and his party had placed the country under the despotic rule of the Puritan and the negro. (Great applause.) He told them that, in order to deserve the lasting confidence of the people, the party must do something besides prepare for election. I tell them that, because his party has done nothing, it cannot have, and will not have the lasting confidence of the American people. He asserted that the past of his party had not been six years. I tell him its future in the State of New York will not be six weeks. (Cheers.) He said in 1861 that the life of the republic was almost extinct. I tell him that it was not so; that the life of the republic still lives, and will live long after he and his party have been consigned to oblivion. (Enthusiastic cheers.) He declared in 1861 that the Treasury of the country was bankrupt; but he failed to call the attention of the people to that splendid condition of its solvency to-day, with three thousand millions of national debt, with five hundred and eighty millions of annual taxation, with interest on that national debt of one thousand millions more than England has to pay, one thousand and eighty millions more than France has to pay; and to the indebtedness of the State of New York, equal to one-third, and more than one-third, of the assessed valuation of its property. The taxation of the State of New York is one hundred and eighty millions of dollars, or forty-five dollars for every man, woman, and child, and two hundred dollars for every voter within the limits of the State. He failed to call the attention of the people to these facts. I call their attention to these facts now, and ask them to remember it in connection with the policy of his party, which the Democratic party of the State is bound to oppose. After he had told them this, to cap the climax he foreshadowed the policy of the party of which he is the representative man, and which is this: That, having added to the power of the Puritan in New England, the power of the illiterate negro in the Southern States, the President of the selection and the election of his own party shall be suspended by joint resolution of Congress, and the Government shall be turned over into new combinations; and then, with a revolutionary President at its head, we shall wade through another revolution without precedent and without parallel!

Gentlemen of the Convention, when in my humble and feeble way I had the honor during the last Fall canvass to discuss the issues of the campaign before the people of the State, I endeavored to show them that the constitutional amendments which were then discussed were not the real issues of the canvass —that they were put forward merely as covers for more dangerous and more destructive schemes. I told them that the real policy of the Radical party in power was what to-day the Convention of Syracuse has itself declared—universal negro suffrage, not only in the Southern States, but in the Northern States—the suspension and impeachment of the President of their own choice, and the putting in his place a President of their own selection. Everywhere I went I was charged by my Radical opponents with making upon that subject partisan harangues, and that the issues of the day were not really as I declared they were. I appeal to the record to show whether the declarations which by myself, and others with me, were then put forth have not been verified by history. They stand to-day where then Butler, and Greeley, and Phillips, and others of that stamp, declared they would stand. The mask and the cover has been thrown off, and the policy so distinctly foreshadowed is the policy that has been announced and avowed by the chairman of that Convention. I do not propose to discuss it here. I am prepared, to the extent of my ability, and my power, and my time, to go among the people and present distinctly to them, in connection with other questions, the issue—Shall the Puritan of New England with the negro of the South rule the destinies of the American country, or shall the country be governed by the people? I leave that for you by your voices to determine. Gentlemen, the difference between the Radical Puritan idea of government and the Democratic idea of government is very marked and very distinct. The Radical Puritan insists upon it that the best government is that which governs the most. The Democrat insists upon it that the best government is that which governs the least. There is the distinction. (Loud applause.) The Radical, acting upon his theory of government, commences his initial policy and allows for no honest difference of opinion. He steps into a Rump Congress and enacts laws which he declares are superior to the Constitution of his country. He insists upon it that his Puritan ideas shall be the dominant ideas of the country, beneath which every other idea shall sink: nothing is so sacred that it must not submit to his wishes. No view, however honest, can be considered honest; no view, however patriotic, can be considered patriotic, if it happen to be at war with his. From the nation it comes to the State, and what then? He declares that the rights of the people of the State, secured to them by the Constitution of the country, shall not be protected and maintained. He declares that the sovereign State of New York shall be regulated by an amendment to the Constitution of the United States; and when the Puritan comes to a Democratic State, that is particularly the place for Puritanic ideas to enter, what then? Odious registry laws, which make a distinction between the adopted citizens and the native citizens, which declare that the adopted citizens shall not be registered, so his vote can be given, unless he produce further evidence of his right to vote than that of citizenship, and which say that papers given under his oath, and which would not be rejected in the courts of this State or anywhere else, shall not be received at the place of registry. Having done that, having raised his voice against adopted citizens of the country by making them a class apart, he goes among them and tells them he is their friend; but he does not stop there. He applies to cities such as New York and Brooklyn—the hearts of the Metropolitan District—a law which I do not hesitate to declare, in its provisions, to be odious, oppressive, harsh, and unjust. He declares what men shall drink, and when they shall drink it. He undertakes to impose upon them his ideas as to how one day shall be spent and how another shall be spent. He makes an odious excise law and intrusts its execution to officers of his own selection, who administer the law with despotic rigor. He intrusts its execution to men who, wherever they go, degrade and disgrace the American character; for a man who plays the part of a spy upon the conduct of an American citizen in his house or place of business degrades himself and disgraces the character of those he represents. (Loud applause.) Having made these laws, laws which are repulsive to the common sense of nearly the whole community; having refused to the Legislature any power to modify them; having provided for their execution in the most repulsive manner, they meet in nominating convention at Syracuse, and at its close pass a resolution by which they seek to escape the consequences of their own acts—a resolution which the journals of the State designate as the "lager-beer resolution"—(derisive laughter)—a resolution. I venture to say, more serious in its character that any of the illicit whiskey that is distilled from the vats of some Radical invaders of the Internal Revenue law. (Great laughter).

I say here that a party which has the control of the legislative and executive power of the State, which has power to amend and modify the laws they find oppressive, harsh, and unjust, cannot escape the responsibility of such legislation. No party in a legislature having the power has any moral right to pass any law which interferes with the life-long habits and customs of the people, which are as harmless as they are universal. (Applause.) I am in favor of just excise laws, with every man within the hearing of my voice. The Democratic party, with all just parties, has been in favor of just and well-regulated excise laws. The object of all laws is to preserve order, and prevent one man doing an injury to his neighbor, and when it has accomplished that its object has ceased, and the law should cease to operate. I insist with you, and I believe that the Democratic party insists with me, that injustice is none the less oppressive because it comes in the form of a law. Now, my friends, there are great questions to be discussed. I can barely allude to them—only to one or two. I have referred to the subject of the national debt, to the immensity of the taxation in the nation and the State. I desire to ask the people of this State, not only the rich who hold the bonds of the government, not only the capitalist whose property is in the State, but every poor man who has his dollar or his hundred dollars deposited in the savings bank, every man who has a home, be it ever so humble, whether he thinks the securities of the government will be worth any more, or taxes upon the people be made any less, if the powers of the Republican party shall be perpetuated? Under the same conditions, I ask the men who hold government securities which are exempt from taxation; I ask men who do not hold government securities, but who pay taxes, whether they think their securities will be worth more or their taxes be less if the country is controlled by the Puritan and negro, with a Revolutionary President at their head, and a Republican Congress? What remedy do you propose, they may ask? I will tell you what I propose. The first is, to oust from power the party who has brought difficulty upon us. (Applause.) It is time enough to give them details when we have the power to execute them. We do not propose—I do not at least—to discuss the question of the national debt. I simply say this to place myself right upon the record. I declare the honor, the good faith of the country is pledged, every dollar of the property of the country is pledged, every right arm of labor in the country is pledged, every energy of the country is pledged to the payment of every dollar of the national debt, honestly and fully, not only according to the letter, but according to the spirit of the bond. (Applause.) It is time enough to discuss the question how it is to be paid, and when it is to be paid, when a party can come in power which can inaugurate a system of economy in the place of a system of extravagance—a party which will give ten independent loyal States back to the Union instead of five military despotisms—(applause)—a party which will develop the resources of the South as well as of the North—which will enable every man in every section of the country to put his shoulder to the wheel and contribute his portion towards the payment of the national debt, and which will relieve the Northern States from the burdens which now rest upon them to pay the whole of it. That is all I propose to say in regard to the national debt, and how it is to be paid, to-day. But I tell the rich and the poor, the old and the young, that it is of no use to pay it, either in gold or in currency, so long as the country is kept comparatively in a state of war. Union, harmony, peace, and restoration is what is needed. Then our securities will become worth their face in gold.

Now, gentlemen, in looking back over the last few years of strife and civil war, I desire to say that I honor every man who, according to his conscientious convictions and the exercise of his judgment and talent which his God has given him, devoted himself to the preservation of the Union which was the common glory of the American people. Our adversaries may claim it to have been the victory of a party ; we know it to have been the victory of a patriotic people. (Applause.) They gave millions from the treasury and hundreds of thousands of lives, and have planted again the American flag in the capital of every State ; they demanded peace, union, harmony, order, law and Constitutional Government. More than two years have elapsed, and they have not obtained either. I appeal to the State, the merchant, the farmer and the laborer, whether to-day we are as near to peace, harmony and prosperity as we were one year ago ? An immense volume of paper currency has corrupted the people ; commerce is declining ; American shipping is destroyed ; the nation is groaning under the heavy burden of debt and taxation. The power of the Legislature is transferred to the military, and the Constitution is no longer the law of the land. Extravagance rules in the nation and in the States. We have no peace, and, as long as the party now in power is continued in its supremacy, we will have no peace. Gentlemen may cry " Peace ! peace ! but there is no peace." In our own State we have had a Legislature which, if common report is to be believed, is full of corruption without precedent and without parallel. Frauds perpetrated in regard to the canal contracts and canal management have been spread before the people in such manner as to astound them. The Radical party controlling the Constitutional Convention have frittered away the time and money of the people, and have refused to submit questions which they made issues before the people, and have adjourned to save themselves from the disgrace which would come upon them, coming out in the beginning, as they did, the avowed advocates of negro suffrage in the States. Within a week of the meeting at Syracuse they voted down the proposition to submit the question to the people. All we ask is to let it go before the people, and, so far as I am concerned, to let it go before the people without discussion and without argument. They refuse to do this, and they must take the consequences. I rejoice in the spirit which seems to animate the members of this Convention, not only as manifested here, but in the interviews I have had the pleasure to hold with them. It gives evidence of a determination which I cannot but admire, which tells of an earnest campaign, to be followed by a great and glorious victory. I feel confident every member of this Convention will so shape his course in the adoption of resolutions, and in the selection of candidates, that personal feelings and prejudices shall give way, that all may labor for the common good, and the result will be that before the lapse of autumn that party, which for its corruption, its extravagance, its folly, and its recklessness, is without precedent and without parallel, will be displaced. (Prolonged applause.)

On the 30th of October, at an enthusiastic ratification meeting of the Democracy, at Morrisania, Westchester county, Mayor Hoffman was present and delivered one of the most marked and effective speeches of the campaign. He commenced by referring to the issues in the State, and then treated in a masterly manner the effect of the Radical legislation and the so-called reconstruction measures of Congress upon the South. From that he passed to the question of negro voting, which he handled in the following manner :

There have been elections lately in Virginia, and when I opened the *New York Tribune* the first thing that greeted me was this great line, "All hail, Virginia!" It seems that the Republicans carried their ticket by 30,000—all negro votes! "All hail, Virginia!"—they may well rejoice while they can. But what will the *Tribune* say when on the morning of the 6th November the returns of this State show that there is a Democratic majority of 30,000? (Laughter and cheers.) What an immense white vote that will be to echo back the vote of Virginia. (Applause.) I want the white man of the North to look at these facts; and I am talking with men who own the State and rule the State, and who I hope will own the State and rule the State forever. (Cheers.) Have you read the accounts of those elections in Virginia, which were secured by the votes of black men—or black men hurried on by white men living down there who could not make an honest living in the States to which they originally belonged? Have you seen how in Richmond the victorious black men told white men that they must leave the State or take the consequences? Have you seen the accounts of how, at the polling places, the leaders of the Radical party handed folded tickets to the negroes, and when a black man was asked, "How did you vote?" he replied, "Dunno; I put in a piece of paper he gim' me!" (Cheers and laughter.) Have you seen how that, while there is a very strict registry law in the State of New York, there was no registration of those negro voters that elected Hunnicutt? Have you a recollection of those facts; and if you have tell us, white men, what sort of a party is this Radical party which allows such things. And tell us whether these plans of theirs will meet with the favor of the men of New York. (Sensation.) Something more than this. This question of negro suffrage at the South is something more than a mere question whether the Radical party shall succeed in controlling Southern elections—it is a question not only affecting Southern States, it is a question affecting the whole country. Go down to the city of New-York and ask the merchant how trade is; ask him whether he has opened accounts with the people of those ten Southern States. He will tell you "No." Ask him if he has opened any new accounts with those new men down there, to control the negroes, upon whom a Radical Congress has conferred the right of voters and the right to govern those States. He will tell you "No." Ask him whether these are the men to purchase goods and develop the resources of the States. He will tell you "No." The merchants are doing nothing with those men—nor any business with those States. And what is the effect of all this? Why, the effect of it is that while you men of the North are doing nothing—while you laboring men up here are at work from early in the morning until late at night to raise money to pay your taxes and the interest on the national debt—a large part of your taxes goes to support a military government in those Southern States, and a Freedmen's Bureau, the chief object of which is to feed the negroes and see how they vote. (Cheers and laughter.)

The other night, at a place where I was speaking, a man called out to me to say something about the eight-hour law. Well, I have but a single word to say about it. So long as the people of the country will encourage and sustain a policy which throws on the white man of the North the whole burden of paying the taxes to sustain these military governments and this Freedmen's Bureau—so long as they do that, it is not worth while to discuss about eight hours' or ten hours' labor, for very soon you will have to work twenty hours. (Sensation and applause.) Now I want you to just look at this thing. There is more money spent to-day to sustain the Freedmen's Bureau than the entire annual expenses

of the Government during the Presidency of John Quincy Adams. I shall
doubtless be told, " Oh, that was a good while ago." Well, let it be ever such
a long while ago, I hope it won't be long before that expenditure will cease.
This Freedmen's Bureau ! why, what is it ? Why, our Radical friends, in Congress and out of it, have asserted that the negro is the equal of the white
man ; and accordingly they have conferred upon him the right of suffrage ; and
the Freedmen's Bureau is to see that he votes correctly. Now, if he needs to be
taught how to vote, he cannot be fit to have the vote. Why, you white men of
the North, you don't need to be fed, and clothed, and taught how to vote for
the Government. (Cheers.) You feed yourselves, don't you ? Yes, and you vote
for yourselves ; and you don't want anybody taxed to help you do that. But there
is more money spent to-day than it cost to carry on the expenses of the Government in John Quincy Adams' time, merely to clothe and maintain the freed negroes
in the Southern States, and secure their votes for the Radical ticket. Do the
men who own ten dollars, or one hundred dollars, or one hundred thousand dollars, think there is any more security given to the finances of the country by
conferring the balance of power upon these men just freed from slavery ? or
does anybody think it will add to the dignity or honor of the Senate of the
United States by sending thither Hunnicutt of Virginia, or Brownlow of Tennessee. (Cries of " No, no !" and applause.) The speaker then referred to recent Democratic victories in Pennsylvania and elsewhere, and an allusion to the
resolutions passed at the Republican Convention at Syracuse, where, he said,
under the term " impartial suffrage " was delicately veiled the Radical policy
of creating a negro balance of power. He proceeded : The next time I took up a
paper I saw there and then the proposition submitted—and I refer to it, although
it has no connection with this branch of my subject, to show the spirit which
animates this Radical party—and that was another amendment to the Constitution of the United States to enforce in every State of the Union a simple local
law which happens to suit Massachusetts and Maine. . . . But, if the men
who control the administration had had the statesmanship and courage to have
conducted public affairs so that all the States would be back in the Union at the
present time they might be deserving of thanks ; but though they have had all
the power and all the money the people could give them, yet two years and
a half after the war is closed the Union is yet not restored. You are more op-
pressed with taxation, borne down by burdens, and overcome by discourage-
ments, than you were when Lee surrendered to Grant. (Cheers.) Now, what
about this debt ? There is an aggregate of annual taxation in the State of
New York of $180,000,000, when you come to take into consideration the State,
local, and national taxation. Now, how much of that do you suppose, apportioned among the voters of the State, would be the amount falling to each voter,
if it were equally distributed per man ? Two hundred dollars to every voter of
the State ; and forty-seven dollars for every man, woman, and child in the State,
two hundred dollars for every voter, and one hundred and eighty millions altogether. Now, that is a pretty serious question. (Applause.) I don't believe
that fact has been mentioned in any Radical meeting in Westchester county this
year. (Laughter; " No.") But there is the debt and there is the tax, and you
have got to pay it and pay the taxes. There is but one way of obtaining relief.
How are we going to do it ? Not by repudiation. Thank God, the Democratic
party never repudiated its honest obligations yet ! (Cheers.) During the war
the Republican administration in the State and country repudiated an honest
debt. Governor Seymour urged upon the Legislature of the State that under

no circumstances should they fail to pay every dollar of the interest on their State debt in gold, as they had agreed to do. (Cheers.) He begged and implored them to stand by the honor of the State, and they refused to do it. Congress declared that a piece of paper, which bore the imprint of Government and the faces of some of the Government officers upon it, was worth just as much as gold; but the people never believed it—(laughter)—and they declared that it should be received as legal tender for all debts, except interest on the public debt. They even passed a law making it a penal offence for any one to sell a gold dollar for more than a paper dollar. That was Radical repudiation during the war. The Democratic party never repudiated an honest obligation, and never will. (Cheers.) It is not the fashion of the honest laboring men, of whom the Democratic party is mostly composed, to refuse to pay a just debt which they owe to anybody. (Cheers.) It has got to be paid. Now, there are a large number of States in the Union; so many that I have almost forgotten how to count them; and it is easier for the whole number of them to pay that debt than for part of them to do it. It is better that the ten States which are kept out of the Union should have a hand in paying it. As it is now, they cannot pay a dollar. They are kept under the rule of a Radical Congress, and there are no results of their labor. Let the Government admit these States to a condition which will build up their business; let it reduce its expenses; stop maintaining an army in the Southern States; stop maintaining the Freedmen's Bureau; stop enabling national banks to get rich out of the interest on the national bonds; cut down the office-holders, and millions of dollars will be saved to the Treasury, and instead of having $200 to every voter in the State of New York to pay, you would bring it down in a little while $100; and instead of $47 to each man, woman, and child, it would be brought down to half that. Our burdens would be lightened, and there would open before us a career of prosperity unparalleled in the history of the country.

On the 28th of February Mayor Hoffman delivered an address at the fourth anniversary meeting of the Working-women's Protective Union of the city of New York. His remarks on this occasion showed that he had carefully studied the condition of this large class in the metropolis, that he fully understood their trials and difficulties, and that he was in thorough sympathy with the aims and struggles of the laboring classes.

His speech was full of practical suggestions and encouragement, and indicated his earnest desire to promote friendly relations between the employer and the employed, and to secure for the latter more satisfactory compensation for their toil, and success in all their efforts to improve their condition.

In October, 1867, Mayor Hoffman attended the *Ledger* banquet in Philadelphia, at which nearly four hundred editors were present, and spoke of the mission of the press, its influence, and its power, and then alluded to its capacity for evil in the following language:

I tell you he who forgets the difference between the liberty of the press and the license of the press, who assails private character, scoffs at religion, gives currency to falsehood, panders to the worst passions of mankind, goes with the public current whichever way it runs, encourages licentiousness, advertises all manner of evil, and circulates libels, may not have visited upon him the terrors and penalties of the human law ; but society will set its mark upon him, and, even while it tolerates and takes his paper, will shun him in his daily life, and leave him to pass through the world without a friend, and into eternity without regret.

CHAPTER VIII.

RE-ELECTION AS MAYOR.

In his speech at the State Convention in October, Mayor Hoffman predicted that New York city would give sixty thousand majority for the ticket that would be nominated there. The returns of the election more than fulfilled that prediction, and the moment that the result was known throughout the State, the Democratic papers in all sections urged upon the Democracy of the city to nominate Mr. Hoffman as their candidate for Mayor. The *World* also came out in a strong article in his behalf. In fact, the rank and file of the party in the metropolis demanded his re-nomination.

On the Saturday evening following the State election, the Tammany Convention assembled at Masonic Hall in Thirteenth street, for the purpose of making the nomination. An immense concourse of people gathered round the building. The street was packed with human beings in every direction. There was but one sentiment manifested by this immense crowd, and that was the nomination of Mr. Hoffman. So earnest were they in his behalf that they could brook no delay, and manifested great impatience for the Convention to organize and proceed to business.

The Convention was finally organized, and John T. Hoffman re-nominated without a dissenting voice. This result was soon announced to the impatient crowd waiting in the street, who greeted the announcement with cheer after cheer.

Mr. Hoffman was immediately sent for, was introduced to the Convention, and briefly addressed them on the issues in this contest, referring to the manner in which the Radicals had taken power away from the people of this city and given it to expensive commissions.

The opponents of Mr. Hoffman in this race were Fernando Wood, the Mozart candidate, and Wm. A. Darling, the Republican. The contest was between Hoffman and Wood, and the canvass exhibited considerable spirit. The *Tribune* and *Herald* heaped upon Mr. Hoffman all the abuse that was within their power. The Democracy in every ward were alive with excitement, and Mr. Hoffman spoke to the people in every section of the city.

They had an opportunity to see more of him, to obtain better personal knowledge of his appearance, manners and habits than on any former occasion. The result of the election tells better than words can describe it the impression that he made upon their minds.

In his speeches during this contest he told the people that he should ask them for their support and their vote in 1868, as he then intended to be again in the field as a candidate for Governor.

As already stated, the Republican candidate, Darling, was practically out of the count. The hopes of the Radicals were fixed upon Wood, and they aided him with all the power they could secretly command. No doubt they would have openly supported him if they had not feared the reaction of such a movement in their own party.

So forcible and convincing were all of Mr. Hoffman's arguments, that they impressed the people with the sincerity of his intentions to administer the municipal government of the metropolis in a satisfactory manner.

The election took place December 3d, and the result is briefly and significantly told by the following figures :

Hoffman's vote..	63,031
Wood's vote...	22,830
Darling's vote	18,559
Hoffman over Wood....................................	40,201
Hoffman over Darling.................................	44,472
Hoffman over all......................................	21,642
Democratic majority in November......................	59,666
Democratic majority in December......................	67,302
Increase in one month................................	7,636

By this handsome and flattering result, Mr. Hoffman enjoyed the distinction of having received the largest majority for Mayor that New York city ever gave for a candidate. In addition to that, he received what no other candidate for that office ever did—a handsome majority in every ward, and in every ward but two or three a majority over both of his competitors.

Mayor Hoffman's fourth annual message to the Common Council was characterized by substantially the same suggestions in regard to necessary changes in the affairs of local government which distinguished his previous messages.

On the evening of January 6th, a large meeting was held in Albany, in pursuance of a call to protest against the action of the British Government with reference to the imprisonment of adopted citizens. The following letter from Mayor Hoffman was read, amid great enthusiasm :

MAYOR'S OFFICE, NEW YORK, Jan. 5.

GENTLEMEN: I have received this day your invitation to attend a mass meeting to aid the Irish revolutionists now battling for liberty, to be held at Union Square on to-morrow evening, at 7½ o'clock. I am aware that it is somewhat the custom of public men to approach the Fenian movement with a delicate regard for our neutrality obligations and of the duties enjoined by the law of nations. Apart from my sympathy for the cause of Ireland, I may be pardoned if I do not individually entertain any very high estimate of Great Britain's claims on us to keep peace with her dominions. When we were struggling for national existence, and the cause of republican government was on its great, perhaps final, trial, England gave aid and comfort—in violation of every principle of neutrality—on the side which it believed would work the destruction of our free institutions. Her people gave sympathy, money, ships and men, and munitions of war, to be used against us.

I do not counsel, nor will I countenance, any violation of the laws of our country ; but I do not stand alone in this community in feeling no very keen sense of our national obligation to England, and an indisposition to go out of my way to seek safeguards for her protection.

At all events, I feel no restraint in expressing, as an American citizen, my most earnest sympathy in the struggle which is now taking place in Ireland, and my hope in its ultimate success.

In the earlier days of the Republic, our Government did not stand on ceremony in expressing its sentiments in behalf of struggling nations emerging into freedom. More than forty years ago, when Greece was battling for liberty against the domination of the Turks, President Monroe did not hesitate to make their cause a subject of a message to Congress, and to express the " strong hope long entertained, founded on the heroic struggle of the Greeks, that they would succeed in their contest and re-assume their equal station among the nations of the earth ;" and later, the Congress of the United States did not hesitate to express its sympathy for the fallen fortunes of the revolutionists of Hungary, and to tender an asylum in this country to Kossuth and his gallant followers.

Should we hesitate to send words of cheer and encouragement, and more substantial aid to the men who are now fighting for the redemption of their native land, because that land is not Hungary, or Poland, or Greece, but Ireland, and the oppressor is not Austria, Russia, or Turkey, but England ?

To my mind, the ultimate success of the people of Ireland in establishing their rights is a certainty. It is impossible that a nation of men of courage and capacity, firmly united in the determination to be free, can long be held in the chains of servile subjection. Ireland demands the restitution of its ancient right of self-government ; that it shall no longer be under the yoke of a power alien in religion, in feeling, in interest ; it demands freedom, equality, and the rights which belong to manhood.

If our Government proves anything, it proves that these demands are just and right, and our history certainly indicates the validity of revolution. But it should be borne in mind that revolutions which do not turn backward are successful revolutions. Unsuccessful revolutions rivet the chains of despotism and give a long day to the oppressor. I know not what may be the means of the men in Ireland or whether this is the fitting opportunity to strike the blow. To give the onward word of command in such a crisis of destiny to a people involves the gravest responsibility.

Let us hope that they who are charged with the responsibility have acted wisely and well, and unite in earnest prayer for an early, successful and happy solution of the troubles of a long-suffering people.

Regretting that the brief time allotted prevents a more elaborate reply.

I am, very respectfully,   JOHN T. HOFFMAN.

We have thus far given several speeches by Mr. Hoffman, which show his political views and his character as a public man. We now give his speech at the New England dinner, in December, 1867, which gives an insight into his social characteristics, and shows his ready appreciation of and participation in the elements of humoristic discourse:

MR. PRESIDENT AND GENTLEMEN: I am exceedingly obliged to you for the very cordial greeting you have given me, and for the toast which has just been read to the city of New York. It has been read without comment or ornamentation. (Laughter.) Whether it is supposed by the New England Society that I am the ornament and commentary of the city (laughter) my Knickerbocker modesty would not permit me to inquire. If I were a New Englander—judging from what I have heard here to-night—I should, in the true spirit of New England, modestly—(laughter)—assert that I was a living representation of the truth that the people of New York are able to govern themselves. (Cheers and laughter.) I must confess that I do not feel entirely at home here. (Loud laughter.) I find when I get into a New England church that I hear always a remarkable mixture of piety and politics. (Laughter.) I find when I come to a New England dinner an equally remarkable mixture of politics and pastry. (Continued laughter.) I can digest the piety and pastry—although they, even, are pretty hard to digest sometimes, according to my ideas—but I have a constitutional aversion to some of the politics, and I must be allowed to express it. (Laughter and applause.) I do it, of course, with all respect to the great mass of the people who are within the sound of my voice, and I should be sorry if anything I should say should tone them down at all, after the very extravagant and extreme laudations I have heard of New England; but I must be permitted to look at things from my own stand-point. My friend, Mr. Beecher—I think I may call him so, for we have never had occasion to quarrel much with each other—says that Yankees in New York have a hard time of it. Well, I don't see why they are permitted to live here. That is some consolation to them. (Laughter.) They are permitted to enter upon all branches of trade and commerce here and make pretty much all the money that is made here, and that is a great consolation to them. (Loud laughter and cheering.) They are permitted to express their sentiments very freely here, and that, with their notions of individual liberty, is a still greater consolation to them (cheers), and they are permitted at a New England dinner at a French restaurant to eat pork and beans, which is no more like the pork and beans of their ancestors than is the luxurious style in which they live here like the simple style in which their ancestors lived in old New England. (Loud laughter and applause.) Now, if these things be all true, how can the Rev. Mr. Beecher—as he is an advocate of truth in so many cases—how can he stand up here and say that the Yankees have a hard time in New York? I have listened with great pleasure to his remarks. He has talked about the great ideas of the Puritans, about their opinions of the rights of conscience, and how they impress truth and morality upon the world. So they do—(cheers) —their own notions of it. (Uproarious laughter.) And yet I cannot forget— and certainly there is no heresy in quoting a New England writer upon New England men—that it has been said that the Puritan's idea of hell was a place where everybody was allowed to think as he pleased. (Laughter.) Now, in saying what I have said, and in quoting what the New England writer says, I think I say nothing disrespectful to the Puritan character of the New England element in our nation. They have their own notions and opinions, and I am sorry to say, from my stand-point, they have had a very unhappy way of enforcing them upon the country. But I hope the time will come, and I believe it is coming, when they, with all the rest of the people of this country, will concede the right of every man to think as he pleases and act as he pleases, provided that in his thinking and acting he does not interfere with the public order and the rights of person and property. (Applause.)

Now, perhaps I ought to stop, but I am not going to. (Laughter and voices, "Go on;" "Go on.") My friend, the President here, intended I should stop at about this point, for he gave me a very bold hint in the course of his remarks. He knew I was a Knickerbocker, and that is what he meant when he said the old Holland maxim was that "speech was silver, but silence was gold." It may be that he meant it for the President of the St. Nicholas Society; if so, he will be able to defend the Knickerbockers of that society. My friend Choate, who has made a very happy and eloquent speech to-night, as he always does, has advanced some new views of reconstruction, which pleased me immensely. (Applause.) He spoke of the times when New England men will go to live in the South, and will take with them their pianos, among other things. I sincerely hope when they take that property down there they won't take any which they originally brought from there during the war—according to popular rumor. (Great laughter.) In the present disorganized condition of the Southern States—with the courts in, to say the least, a very bad condition, notwithstanding that my old friend, Judge Busteed, is down there administering the law, and replevin suits may be plenty, although judgments may be doubtful—I would suggest that instead of taking their pianos they take their tuning-forks. (Laughter.) Now, gentlemen, some allusions have been made to my constituents in New York—not very respectful allusions, I think, to my Irish constituents. General Sickles has referred to the fact that when we get Ireland for the Alabama claims we shall be able to get offices for all your Irish friends who desire them. (Laughter.) I am free to say, gentlemen, that that would be a very great relief to me. (Loud laughter.) And it affords another reason why I shall always insist, as I do now insist, that the Alabama claims shall be settled and the rights of American citizens, adopted as well as native, shall be protected everywhere. (Applause.) But while allusions have been made to my Irish constituency and my Irish friends, justice has not been done to them. The President of the St. Patrick's Society is not here, and therefore I must make a slight reference to the fact that they have contributed to the wealth and the greatness of this country. They have built its railroads and canals; and in that connection I beg leave to call attention to the fact that the only canal I ever knew to be dug out by a New Englander was the Dutch Gap (great laughter), and that was not a very great success. If his notions of repudiation are not more perspicuous than his notions of canal building I think they will prove as great a failure. (Cheers.) Now, my friends, I have only a single word more to say. You can see from what I have already said that I did not come here prepared to make a speech. I have relied entirely on the subjects furnished by the speakers who have preceded me. I ought not to sit down without saying one word about the city which I represent. Two years ago I had the honor to be the guest of the New England Society. It was a great dinner and an enthusiastic company; and it was just subsequent to an important contest in which I had been elected to the Chief Magistracy of my city. I said then that during the two years of my term I hoped I should prove myself to be a Mayor not only of the party, but of the city. I trust I have kept my word. (Loud applause.) If I have I am glad to be here to-night. I am glad to be hear to-night as the representative of a city, the great majority of the people of which hold political opinions differing from those of the majority of the persons before me, but who are true to the Union, the Constitution, and the laws—the greatest city on the American continent, and destined in time, as I believe, to be the greatest city in the world. (Cheers.) And one secret of its greatness and success is that within its narrow boundaries you find all nationalities, people of all sections and all States, who come together with their wealth, their enterprise, and their energy, not only for the advancement of their own personal interests, but for the development of the greatness of that great State of which they become citizens and in whose prosperity they take great pride. During the war the city of New York, whatever may have been said against it and its people, furnished more money and gave more men to support the Union of the States than any other city in proportion to its population in the State or country. (Applause.) When men were wanted they were called for and furnished here. When the Government was in pecuniary distress, calls were made upon the bankers, and merchants, and capitalists of New York, and the money flowed lavishly into the public treasury. If during that struggle there were signs of things here which were unfavorable to the Government, there was always the great mass of the earnest, patriotic people ready to put them down; and the people showed themselves to be devoted heart and soul to that Union and that Constitution which they believed to be the common glory of all. And the city thus still keeps up to its reputation; it still stands by the country, by the Union and Constitution, and it looks forward to the time when the feeling of true brotherhood shall be established between all sections of the land, and the time when partisan spirit shall give way to patriotic impulses—when parties shall be buried under the dust, and when statesmen shall rise above the surface. God speed the time! Let it come quickly; and before another New England assemblage gathers here to celebrate this anniversary day may the time come when every State in this Union shall be back in its old place under the Constitution of the country, and every star shall be a representative of the State in the flag, and when the war and all its memories which are painful and unpleasant shall have passed away from the minds of men. (Tremendous cheering.)

DEFENCE OF THE PRESIDENT.

On the evening of February 28, a great mass meeting was held at Cooper Institute for the purpose of arraigning the Radical leaders in Congress for their revolutionary schemes and proposed impeachment of the President. Mr. Hoffman's speech was as follows:

MY FELLOW-CITIZENS: I am not among the invited speakers to-night. I did not come to make a speech. I came intending to be a silent member of this vast assemblage; but I came by my humble presence to be among those who wish to make earnest protest against a grievous wrong—(applause)—the perpetration of which is being threatened in the capital of our country. But if I am to speak at all, I wish it understood that I speak not as a partisan—I am not here as a partisan—I am here as an American citizen. (Loud applause.) I claim to be here, also, as the head of an American city—(applause)—which numbers among its population 100,000 hardy, sturdy men, who to-morrow would cast their ballots in support of every word I shall utter here this night. (Applause.) This meeting has been called by merchants and bankers and professional men in this great commercial city, who represent its capital to the extent of millions upon millions of dollars. It is well it has been done. It would have been a shame and a disgrace to the American nation if no voice went forth from its great commercial emporium at a time when a partisan majority in Congress were attempting to overthrow the President of the United States under the mere form of law. (Great applause.) It is well that it is so, for it would be a burning shame, a disgrace to the civilization of the age, if the men of this great city, and interested as they are in the success and prosperity of the whole country, uttered no word of censure and condemnation of that partisan act of a partisan majority in the two houses of Congress. (Applause.) What is it all about? A very simple story; a story, however, which every man should read and understand; a simple story which, I regret to say, every man has not read and every man does not understand. I venture to say now that within one mile of this spot can be found the counting houses of men who transact, every day of the year, business to the amount of millions of dollars, who have not even read the communication which the President of the United States sent to the Senate, explaining the act which he did when he removed Mr. Stanton and appointed General Thomas Secretary *ad interim*. And inasmuch as they have not read it, and inasmuch as there are many in this city who have not yet understood this question now before the American people, it is well that we should stop and see just what it is. This is no time for passions, nor for idle declamation. This is a serious time in the history of the American nation. Mr. Johnson, President of the United States, was elected to power by the party which now denounces him. I am not here as his advocate or his champion. He has done much which I applaud; he has omitted to do much for which I censure him. He is the President of the United States by virtue of its Constitution; not the acting President, filling out Mr. Lincoln's term of office, but the President of the United States by virtue of the Constitution. (Applause.) From the earliest history of the Government the President has chosen his Cabinet. Never has there been an exception to that proposition. Mr. Johnson coming into office upon the death of Mr. Lincoln, retained in office temporarily certain members of that Cabinet. Mr. Stanton holds a commission which has been read to you to-night, issued by President Lincoln in 1862, designating him as Secretary of War during the pleasure of the President, for the time being. Differences have arisen in the Cabinet. It is no longer profitable or pleasant for the President of the United States to have in his Cabinet a man with whom he may have no communication; a man who is at war with him, his ideas, and his policy. What does he do? He requests him to resign. Mr. Stanton declines. Senators in Congress, members of the House of Representatives, when the Civil Tenure bill was under discussion, stated upon the floor, and no man was bold enough to deny it, that it was hardly to be supposed that any gentleman, any man of honor, would be found who would desire to stay in the Cabinet of the President if he expressed a wish that he should leave. (Laughter and applause.) It seems—I was going to say—that they were mistaken. (Renewed laughter.) But perhaps they were not. (Cheers.) It depends entirely upon whether the present so-called Secretary of War, Mr. Stanton, comes within either of the classes mentioned by the Senators in this debate. (Laughter and cheers.) But Mr. Stanton declined to go, and the President did what? He issued an order for his removal, and designated a General in the army to take his place until a successor should be confirmed, and he nominated his successor. He offered no force, no resistance to any law, whether the law be constitutional or not. There was no attempt at resistance, nor disturbance; a mere exercise of the power always exercised by the President of the United States and never denied to him, and that exercise, too, for the purpose of having the question decided before the proper tribunals, whether he had a right to exercise it or not. The President had taken an oath to support the Constitution of the country, and to maintain and defend it. Can he not do it by appealing to the courts for redress—for a judgment upon the construction or the constitutionality of the law? That is all he has done. What then? Why, my friends, in less time than it would take to draw a declaration upon a promissory note and have it served within the limits of New York, one house of Congress, by a purely party vote, with two exceptions, voted to impeach the President of the United States for a high crime and misdemeanor.

Now, what is the law? Mr. Girard has fully explained it. But one single word upon it. That point of the Civil Tenure bill which forbade the President removing from office those who hold office by virtue of his appointment and confirmed by the Senate, says that they shall hold office during the term of the President by whom they were appointed, and for one month thereafter, subject to the advice and consent of the Senate. The President has undertaken to remove no Cabinet officer appointed by himself and confirmed by the Senate. He simply undertakes to remove a Cabinet officer appointed by his predecessor, and who refused to do what members of the Congress now supporting him said no gentleman or man of honor would decline to do. I am free to say that when I see so great an agitation built up on so slight a foundation I am amazed. It cannot be otherwise. What does it all mean? Recollect that this Congress has been seeking for a long time some ground upon which to impeach the President. Within three weeks, I think I may say, a majority of the Committee in the House had voted seven to two, I think, against impeachment; and there was a declaration almost unanimous that up to that time the President of the United States had done nothing which deserved impeachment. Very well; if he had done nothing then, the only thing is the order removing Stanton, and substituting in his place a General of the army. Is it any wonder, now, that the 22d of February—which should have been devoted to a nobler purpose than seeking to depose the

President—that the passion which characterized these men on that day has now cooled down, and that they are hesitating as to what kind of articles to prefer ? (Laughter and cheers.) Is it strange that the telegraphic dispatches and the papers announce that the trial will possibly last longer than was expected ? Is it to be wondered that when Mr. Stanton's commission from President Lincoln sees the light for the first time since it was written, that these men should begin to ask themselves whether they are not in a little difficulty in this case ? (Laughter.) My friends, I tell you there can be only one reason for having that impeachment proceeding pressed in the Senate of the country, and that is that the Radical party are determined to get control of the Presidency in advance of the election. (That's it.) I venture a prophecy, if this thing goes through. I venture to prophesy, not in regard to members of the House of Representatives merely, but in the aggregate, that this movement will stand forth in history as one of the few, or one of the many things if you please, which have disgraced the present century, though its individual movers will be forgotten. But I speak in regard to the Senators who are to sit as judges upon the President, one of whom says he represents the great commercial interests of New York city and State. I will speak with prophecy, that the nomination of one President and the impeachment of another will stand side by side upon the pages of history, alike odious and infamous in the eyes of the civilized world. (Tremendous applause.) A few words more, my friends, and I have done. (Cries of "Go on, go on.") Who is the chief assailant in the House ? (Voice— "Thad. Stevens.") Who is it, with his trembling frame and hoary head, with one foot in the grave, that is borne into the Senate to present charges ? He who, standing upon the record of his oft-repeated declarations, that the policy of Congress, of which he had been the chief advocate, was outside, above and beyond the Constitution of the country. He who, having taken oath to support the Constitution of the country as a member of the American Congress, boldly avows that the measures for which he has voted and which he has supported are outside of the Constitution and in violation of it. He is the chosen man of the House of Representatives to appear before the bar of the Senate and prefer charges against the President of the United States for resisting the laws of the country ! Will the business men and merchants of this city and country recollect this ? Our Government has stood the test of peace and war pretty well. The President in the hour of trial has at all times been sustained by the people. The Congress has had its share of public support. But the fact has always been recognized that the executive, the legislative and the judicial departments were distinct and independent, and that the safety of the whole country rested upon this fact. If the business men of New York and of America do not rise and remonstrate against the attempt of Congress to seize upon the executive office by the vote of a mere party majority in it, then farewell to the Constitution and farewell to liberty ! (Applause.) The removal of Mr. Johnson, per se, might affect the Government's credit and the Government's peace. I hope it would not. The removal of Mr. Lincoln by the hands of an assassin did not affect the credit or security or peace of the Government. But that is no reason why assassination should be imitated. And although the removal of Mr. Johnson, per se, as Andrew Johnson, would not strike upon the public mind with fear and terror, nevertheless, the fact that a party majority in Congress attempt to remove the President of the United States ought to make them tremble. Precedents are dangerous things sometimes. The time may come when such a course would be followed with disaster. Men all through this country, rich and poor, are to-day discussing the question how the national debt is to be paid, whether in gold or in currency. Let me tell them, and let me say to the bankers and business men of New York, that unless they frown down this first attempt of Congress to eject a President without a cause, they had better ask themselves the question what security they have got in the great future that it will be paid at all. (Cries of "Good," and cheers.) Once destroy the landmarks of your Government; once cast off the great anchors which have held you firm and fast; once let it be understood that one branch of the Government can be overridden and overpowered by another, if they happen to come in political collision; once let it be understood that the Constitution of the country is not the supreme law of the land, but that the will of the party majority in Congress is—let me ask the capitalists of New York where is the security for your personal interests or your personal liberty? (Applause.) I protest, therefore, against these partisan acts. As a party man, as an earnest member of the Democratic party—(applause)—occupying some prominence, perhaps, in its council, and looking at that impeachment in Washington as a party question, I would not protest; I would say let it go on; because I know, as well as I know anything in the future, the effect that it will produce upon the politics of the country, assuming that we are to have free elections. But, rising above the partisan, as an American citizen, as a member and citizen of the great city of New York, as the head of that city which has to-day 100,000 men who would vote to-morrow as one man against this act of Congress. I protest against it; and I warn these people in Congress and throughout the country to pursue this act no further. There will be no resistance by force. But the greatest force in any civilized age is the force of public opinion expressed as the people know how to express it. (Applause.) I only know that the President of the United States stands now in Washington as it were alone. Cabinet members are forced upon him against his will. Majorities in Congress are denouncing him, and threatening impeachment. He stands there, however, the representative of the Presidential office, bound to defend its integrity and its prerogatives. And the arm of the public is with him, and will sustain him. (Loud applause.) My friends, as I told you, I came here not intending to say a word; I have said but little more, perhaps, than I should. I thank you, not for the attention you have given to me, but for the manifestation you have made of your determination to sustain the Executive of the country in his defence of the prerogatives and the power of his office. (Great applause.)

In the Connecticut campaign of last spring, which resulted so auspiciously for the Democracy, Mr. Hoffman took a leading and influential part. He spoke about six times during the canvass, and always with the same force of argument, terseness of statement and logical language that characterize all his speeches. His speech at Stamford, March 28, was practically the keynote of the campaign of 1868, and is so powerful that we give it in full:

This large assemblage, gathered at the close of a week's labor and care to hear discussed the issues involved in the contest which now occupies the attention of the people of Connecticut and the whole country, these upturned, earnest faces upon which I now look, the enthusiasm with which you greet the speaker, tell me that the people of this State realize to its full extent the importance of the struggle in which they are engaged. It is well that it is so, for it is beyond all question that this is one of the decisive political contests of the century.

occurs in a State not great in its territorial dimensions, but yet great in its wealth, great in its intelligence, great in its earnest educated labor—a State which, taking into account its population, is not equalled, and certainly is not excelled, by any in the American Union. It comes on in the spring-time of the year, just as the snows of winter are melting and the ice giving way to the genial influence of the sun. And it comes at a time, too, when the conservative mind of the country in every portion of its vast extent feels that a period has arrived, when the chilling snows and blasts of war, of passion, of prejudice, of hatred, should vanish before a more genial spring-time in the hearts of the American people. Three years have passed since the deplorable war in which this people were engaged came to a close ; three years have passed since the last gun was fired in that terrible civil strife ; three years have passed since the contending hosts laid down their arms and returned to their homes ; and yet the people of this country are not at peace. My friends, I come among you not to make any appeal to your prejudices or to your passions ; but looking upon you as American citizens interested in the welfare of your country, in the future prosperity of this land, and knowing that you feel—every man and woman among you—that something is needed to make it prosperous and happy different from prejudice or passion ; that what it needs is that the people should look calmly at the questions which divide and distract them and see if there be not some way of escape. Three years, I say, have passed since the war was ended. At that time the people were burdened with an enormous debt, their taxation was heavy, they were divided into two sections, the North and the South, yet they looked forward to a speedy restoration of harmony among them and to a rapid diminution of their burdens. And now, I ask, after three years of peace, in what condition do we find the country ? The debt is as heavy as when the war closed, the taxation is as burdensome as ever it was, there are just as many citizens out of employment, and there is just as much discord and want of harmony as when the cannon of opposing factions were bellowing at each other. The party in power seek to impeach and to overthrow the President of the United States, and they threaten to assume the power to say who shall have the suffrage and who shall not, to tell you people of Connecticut who shall and who shall not vote at your polls. Have we a restored country ? No. Have we a united people ? No. Who is responsible for the present state of things ? Who were in power during the war, and who have been in power since the war ended ? I do not intend to discuss the issues which arose before the war or while it lasted. They ended when General Lee met General Grant and surrendered to him, and their soldiers went home in peace. I stand here to discuss the issues of the present. Who have been in power, I ask, since the war closed ? The Radical party. It has a majority of two-thirds in Congress. It has control over every department of the Government. It has the army. It has the navy. It has had a people ready to sustain them in all they did. They tell us that they have not had control of the executive department of the Government ; that the President has not been in accord with them in their plans for restoring the Union ; that he has been an obstruction to reconstruction ; that he has embarrassed them in every way he could ; that he has prevented the introduction of harmony among the people.

My friends, this is a misrepresentation of the truth. It is true that the President has not been in harmony with them. It is true that he has opposed their revolutionary acts. It is true that he has put his veto upon their unconstitutional bills. But it is not true that he has hindered them from doing what they pleased to do. He has vetoed their bills, but in forty-eight hours thereafter they have repassed them over his veto. He has not been able to prevent the carrying out of any plan or scheme of reconstruction which they have formed. I want to start with this proposition, that the responsibility of the present condition of things rests with them, and them alone, and that they must take it. It will not do for a Radical Congress having a two-third majority to attempt to saddle the responsibility of the condition of the country upon any one but themselves. What is this thing of reconstruction? It is the simplest thing in the world. There is no difficulty about it. I shall not discuss the numerous acts of Congress bearing upon it. It is enough for me to know that the Radical party have been the party in power, and that it has not yet reconstructed the country. The reason is that they do not want to reconstruct it. Their policy has not been to reconstruct the Union for the sake of the Union, but to keep it unreconstructed for the sake of the Radical party. Their policy has not been to get back into the Union those ten States that attempted to go out of it during the war, in the same condition and enjoying the same rights as they enjoyed before the war, but to get them back in such a way that the so-called representatives of the people in Congress might still retain their ill-gotten power; that Congress might represent, not the people of all the sections from which they came, but the people of Massachusetts. Reconstruction is the easiest thing in the world. What is it? Simply this: that when the war was ended, and the question which had been involved in it had by its close been practically settled, the section which had attempted to secede should acquiesce in that which was required by the common consent of all the people that slavery should be at an end, the acts of secession repealed, and the rebel debt be abolished. It was all done, and then there was nothing more to be done than for these Southern States to send to Congress such representatives as it would receive. That was all. If the Southern people chose to send men there who were not the proper persons to send, and men who were not true to the Constitution and laws of the country, Congress had the power to refuse them admission. If after they obtained admission they showed themselves unfit to be representatives, it was in the power of Congress to expel them. There is the whole mystery of reconstruction. But this Radical party in Congress were determined from the outset that these States should not be allowed to be represented in Congress unless they sent representatives who held Radical sentiments, and their policy has therefore been to keep these States out of the Union till that purpose was accomplished. For this purpose they have received representatives from newly created States that had barely population enough to entitle them to representation. Not only that, but they have excluded representatives from other States upon the ground that they were not loyal to the Constitution of the country. Not only that, but they have expelled from the doors of Congress every man who was not a Radical. Shall I give you an illustration? The other day the State of Maryland sent General Thomas to represent them in Congress, and the objection brought to exclude him was, that when his son, against his father's will and entreaty, went to join the rebel army, the General gave him a hundred dollars to keep him from starvation when the time of starvation should come. But when Ben Butler came to claim admittance, although he had been a member of the rebel Congress, he was immediately admitted into the church of the Radical party. Now I propose to take up these questions and to discuss them calmly, plainly, honestly, and to meet the objections made by our Radical opponents to the course the Democratic party propose to adopt. We are told, and this is the argument of the Radical speakers, that the white men of the South are rebels, and, therefore, not fit to be admitted to representation. I would like to ask a question in Radical arithmetic: if three years of Radical legislation has kept these men rebels, how many years will it take to make them good loyal men? (Laughter.) We are told that the Southern people are rebels yet, and that there is, therefore, no hope for the country but to turn those States over to the dominion of the negro population. I was amused, in this connection, to read in the New York *Post*, a Republican paper, a dispatch from a Republican correspondent in the South, that Georgia and South Carolina could be carried by a white Republican majority. If that be true, as our Radical friend says, it shows how popular Radical theories must be getting down there. But, my friends, I do not come here to discuss this question in the interests of the Southern people particularly. I come to discuss it also in the interest of the Northern people. And apart from consideration for the good of the whole people, the next thing is for the people of a section of the country to look at how measures affect themselves. I want you men of Connecticut, who are to vote shortly upon your own representatives in the councils of the country, to consider how this Radical policy of reconstruction is affecting you.

When this war ended, did you not expect that the trade of the country was going to revive again? Thousands of men had been withdrawn from the labor and the manufactures of the country. A large section of the country was closed to our products. This was partially relieved by the demand of the Government for the provisions and munitions necessary for carrying on a great war. But the war was ended, and even this market was closed. The people looked for another and better market in the restored South, now that the Government wanted their industry and products no longer. Has it been so? Has any capital been invested in those States since they submitted to the arms of the North? A company was formed in this State last winter, called the Planters' Loan Aid Association, but it could not get enough to pay for the papers required for its due organization. Thus you see that this Radical policy of reconstruction keeps from you a market that ought to have been reopened to you long ago. Not only this, but unusual and heavy expenses to support the Government are put upon you. You have to support a large standing army in time of peace. You have the navy to keep up; you are compelled to sustain a host of tax-gatherers and office-holders. The question comes home directly to you: Will you defeat and rebuke the policy which causes this state of things to exist? I shall presently discuss more at length this question of taxation and debt, but there are other points to be touched upon first. I have charged already upon this Radical Congress that they have prevented the reconstruction of the Union. I have to charge upon them something more than that. I have to charge upon them that their whole object, if not their avowed, yet their secret object, is to subvert the Union and the Constitution, and they are at work earnestly to effect this object. They have kept the ten Southern States out of the Union for years, and they are now attempting unconstitutionally to take upon themselves the functions of the executive department of the Government. I have a few words to say upon this question of impeachment. I tell you that it is a more important question than you think. Men are deluded by the idea that it affects only one man, while in fact it strikes at the very foundations of the American Government. I heard the other day a man in the business walks of life say, speaking of this question, that if the country could not stand firm under the impeachment of the President, then it was not worth preserving. I tell you that this is a dangerous doctrine. This country stood without a fatal shock the assassination of Abraham Lincoln, but yet that is not a thing to be imitated. Because the country may stand firm under the political assassination of Andrew Johnson, it does not follow that it should be allowed to proceed with indifference. It is a serious business to impeach a President of the United States. This is the first time in our history that it has been attempted: I trust in God it may be the last. I hope, at any rate, that if it ever occurs again there will be some shadow of a pretext for it. I hope it will never occur again upon the dictation of a party majority in Congress, and when the men of the party which impeaches stand and say in private circles that it is wrong. There are those who say that it is not necessary to discuss this question of impeachment, but I feel that I would not be doing my duty to my country or this audience if I failed to discuss it. (Applause.) What does this mean, that the President of the United States is impeached for high crimes and misdemeanors? What is the crime for which this extraordinary, this unprecedented course is taken? It is simply that he issued an order to remove from office Edwin M. Stanton. Is it a high crime and misdemeanor to turn a Radical out of office? If so, Heaven have mercy upon the citizens of this country next Fall; for in my opinion there will be a general turning out of Radical members of both Houses of Congress. A crime to turn Edwin M. Stanton out of office! Do you suppose that it would have been a crime in the eyes of the Radical members of Congress to turn out of office Seward, or any member of the President's Cabinet except Stanton? I think it would be looked upon by most of them rather as a political virtue than as a political crime. In what respect is it a crime? What is the law? The law simply is, that members of the President's Cabinet shall hold office during the term of office of the President that appointed them. And Edwin M. Stanton was appointed, not by Andrew Johnson, but by Abraham Lincoln. But, say these men, Johnson knew just what Congress meant when they passed the Tenure-of-Office Act, that they meant it to apply to those appointed by the latter as well as those appointed by the former—making their intention the rule of conduct instead of their expressed will. I tell you, friends, it is time to attempt to convict the President of high crimes and misdemeanors when it is pretended that he has tried to injure the interests of the American people. What did General Sherman say, in a letter respecting the proposed removal of Stanton from office? He says that he offered to go with General Grant to Stanton and advise him to resign *for the good of the country;* if he would not do so, then it would be time to contrive ulterior measures. Yet the Radical associates of Sherman say that it was contrary to the interests of the country to remove Stanton, and make a test case to try the constitutionality of their act for the holding of offices. And now it is said that they are going to nominate General Grant as the Radical candidate for the Presidency. Yet we call your attention to the fact that Grant, the nominee of the Radical party, was going with Sherman, had he not been prevented, to advise Stanton to resign office for the good of the country, and that the same Radical party are impeaching the President for attempting to remove him for the good of the country.

What, my friends, does this impeachment business mean? It means simply this, and you had better bear it in mind: that though by the Constitution of the country the three departments of the Government, the legislative, the executive, and the judicial, are made independent of each other, yet a Radical majority in Congress which holds its life by that Constitution have assumed the power to turn out the President, who holds his position by the same authority as they do, upon any pretext of party necessity or other, and to name the man who shall take his place. Are you willing to have that precedent established? But what harm will it do, you ask, to remove Andrew Johnson? What harm? What harm can come from overthrowing any great principle? What harm is it to go out to sea without a compass or a chart? What harm is it to ignore the very first principles of our Government? Answer these questions and I will tell you what harm it is to impeach and remove Andrew Johnson without good cause. I ask the business men of this town, I care not whether they be rich or poor, who have money and property invested in the country, what may not come from allowing Mr. Wade to be placed in the Presidential chair,—Mr. Wade, who made that proposition, which none but a demagogue could make, that property should be divided among the people, without reference to those who owned or earned it? This is a fact, and yet men are perfectly indifferent whether Mr. Johnson is deposed or not, and Mr. Wade placed in the Presidential chair. They talk about the national debt; how important it is to make provision for its payment, and to protect the honor and credit of the country, and yet they stand indifferent to the violation of the Constitution, and to the probable elevation to the Presidency of a man who dared to advocate the doctrine that property should be divided without reference to the men who make it and own it. But these Radicals do not stop there, but strike next at the Supreme Court of the country. What care I for that? says some one; I never have any cases there. It is not in my sphere of life. No questions arise in my business that require its action. And men come among you and tell you that it is all well enough to declaim about the Supreme Court, but it is only talk for a purpose. And yet there is not a man in the State of Connecticut who does not know that if his neighbor wrongs him in person or property his only remedy is in the laws and in the courts which administer them, and that if Congress has the right to strike down the law when it pleases he must be at the mercy of his political opponent. How about the matter of the Supreme Court? Under a recent act of Congress, a man having a case involving two dollars may have it taken before the Supreme Court, while matters of life and death are given over to a military organization under the control of a partisan government. I charge upon the Radicals that they dare not submit their acts to the decision of the Supreme Court of the land, constituted under its Constitution. Strike down the courts and where are you? At the mercy of the Radical party? Yes, just now. But that is not the whole. Things may change, and another party be in the ascendant. But whichever is in power, no man's interests are secure if all power rests only in Congress. Look at these men in Congress at the present time; what are they doing? Taking action to convict the President of violation of the law. And who is the chief impeacher? Thaddeus Stevens, who boldly declares that impeachment is to be decided beyond the Constitution and above it, and that Congress may act aside from it. If the Supreme Court stays them in their course, they will not hesitate to suppress that bulwark of American liberty and rights. Consider what this would be if done in your own State. You have a constitution; you have three branches in your government—the executive, the legislative, and the judicial. The wisdom of your fathers told you that this was necessary. Suppose that the Legislature of Connecticut should attempt to abolish one or other branch of the State government; what would the people of the State say to that? They would say to its members. You have been false to the Constitution of the State; you deserve to be hurled from power, and you shall be. (Cheers.) There are within this room men of labor and men of wealth, but there is no division between you on questions of interest; your interest is alike in preserving the Government as your forefathers left it to you. If the Constitution does not provide for new emergencies which arise, there is a way provided in itself for its alteration and amendment. But you are not safe in the hands of people who attempt to act independently of the executive and judicial parts of the Government. But further, my friends, the Radicals have not stopped at keeping out of the Union ten States, with striking down the President or attempting to do it, and with striking down the Supreme Court; but there is another policy which they avow, and which they are attempting to carry into execution.

This policy is what they call an equality of races, equality of the white and black races of this country. They have virtually turned the South over to the control of the negro population there. They have disfranchised the great mass of the white intelligence of the South, and left it virtually in the hands of the blacks. Perhaps I am wrong to say virtually under the control of the blacks, for the blacks are under the complete control of the Freedmen's Bureau which has been established there, and is maintained at public expense and supported by the taxes of the North. Let us look at this question of negro suffrage. You have not chosen it here in Connecticut. You voted it down when it was presented to you directly, and you virtually voted it down again in your last election. The question was of very little consequence comparatively in this State, for your negro population is very small. Yet you opposed it, and the white masses of the North generally rejected it. But notwithstanding, Congress saddles it upon the Southern States, where there are large negro populations, and where it is of great consequence, and where the people are strongly opposed to it. It seems scarcely worth while to argue the question of negro equality and fitness for the suffrage, for no one believes in it. And yet within two years the great body of the Republican party have changed from an attitude of hostility to it to one of the very opposite description. Two years ago, when I predicted that if the Democratic party did not arouse, the South would be placed under a negro domination and the President be impeached, I was laughed at. To-day both have come to pass. How about this equality of races? Have you ever seen it in Connecticut? Have you ever seen it anywhere? Does it exist in the City of Washington? Look at those extreme Radical men who talk about the rights of the negro, and the ability of the negro. Do you find them employing them as clerks or otherwise in any of the departments? Go with me to that city, and where will you find them except on the street-crossings, at boot-black stands, or in the galleries of Congress. The great Thaddeus Stevens himself has no negro in his employ except the man who brushes his clothes or blacks his boots. A gentleman told me lately that he saw in the South a jury of six white men and six black men sitting side by side, and the judge informed him that not one of the latter could either read or write. Is that the way to reconstruct the South? Is that the way to make it great and prosperous? Is that the way to put it in a condition to help pay the debt of the country? Is that the way to help the Southern people? Is that the way to make them good Union-loving, loyal men? My friends, you would not tolerate it for an instant in the State of Connecticut. Can you expect that such a course will make a happy, contented, united people anywhere? But you are told that these people have been freed from slavery and been made citizens, and must have all the rights and protection accorded to citizens. I say so too. Let us do all in our power to better their condition. But if we are not more successful in doing so than we have been in the Northern States for the last half century, may God have mercy upon the country which is ruled by them. (Applause.) I would go as far as any man in helping to elevate their condition, as far as that is possible, but when it comes to giving them the power to govern whole States I do not consent. What do they know about governing States? "Oh," said a Radical with whom I conversed on this subject, "they are just as fit as the Irish or Germans." If they spoke honestly they would tell you that their very object in giving the negroes the right of suffrage was to offset the vote of the Irish and the German citizens. They tell you that the negroes are just as intelligent as the poor whites of the South. That may be; but that is no reason why the government of the South should be given up to the poor whites and the negroes combined. These people, as I have said, are governed by the Freedmen's Bureau. It feeds and clothes them, and controls them. That Bureau is a creature of the Radical Congress at Washington, which thus furnishes employment to Radical emissaries and pays them out of the treasury of the country to rule the South in the interest of the party. The money for all this feeding and clothing and supporting of the Bureau comes out of the people of the North. Their position is this: that if the negroes down South are fit to vote, and assume all the rights of American citizens, they are fit to take care of themselves and pay their portion of the general expenses. (Applause.) But the question is hardly worth argument. There is not a Radical who would say upon his oath that the negroes are fit to have the control of any government in their hands. But they will say in confidence to you that the Radical party have got the control of them, and so they control the South. How do they control them? By sending down to the South a set of people who could hardly earn for themselves a decent living in the North, who hope eventually to be elected to represent it, and then the party will claim that as an expression of the sentiment of the South. This thing must be stopped, and you people of Connecticut must stop it. I say you people of Connecticut, for I tell you that if in this spring election in Connecticut the voice of the people is in favor of the Radical policy, it may be that not only in substance your Government may be destroyed, but you will have saddled upon you this very burden which now the South labors under.

Last winter the Legislature in this State, at the recommendation of Governor English, abolished the poll-tax, so that every man in it could vote. Next year Congress may say that no man shall vote in the State unless he is worth a hundred thousand dollars, or, going further, that you shall not vote unless you are in accord with their political policy. These men say that they represent a majority of the people, and, therefore, their voice is the voice of the people. I say they do not represent a majority of the people. Take the State of New York, for instance. Last year it gave fifty thousand Democratic majority (cheers), and yet it is represented by two Radical Senators and by a large majority of Radical Congressmen. Take the State of California. Last year it gave a Democratic majority in its Legislature, and yet to-day it is represented by Radicals. Ohio last year elected a Democratic Senator who takes his seat in 1869, and yet to-day it is represented by two Radicals, and in the Assembly by a large majority of Radicals. The same is the case in Pennsylvania. The result of the elections in the North so far is that a considerable majority of the votes cast were Democratic, and yet two-thirds of the Congress is Radical; and these men overthrow your forms of government under the pretence that they represent a majority of the people. There never was a more false and monstrous proposition put forth. No argument is brought before the people more popular but more deceptive than this, that the will of a majority of the people is the law of the land, the Constitution to the contrary notwithstanding. I leave the subject to say a few words on the present condition of the North. Is it prosperous? It is not; business is decreasing; commerce is shrinking. Go among your manufacturers. Some of them are doing work, but are there not thousands in Connecticut out of employment? In the great city of New York you will see more clerks gazing out of the windows than customers going into the shops. There are thousands willing to work, anxious to work, longing to work, but they cannot get work. There is no trade with the South, and the demand in the West is limited. Why? Because there is no confidence among the people about their future. Look at the South. Have you heard of any Northern manufacturer opening an account with any of the freedmen of the South, or with any of the whites? Why does not capital go there? Because there is no security for it. The country is under military or negro domination. What Northern man will send his capital or his goods there? And things are getting worse and will get worse, and taxes become more oppressive. Congress has passed a law taking off the internal revenue tax. But if revenue is not collected from manufactures it must be from something else. The Government must have a revenue in some shape or other. There is no dodging this except by repudiating the debt. The fact is, the movement is made only to influence the election in Connecticut, but I do not think it will do it. (Applause.) Everything is taxed except Government securities; and while thousands may be invested in them and be free from taxation, it is wrung out of the labor of the poor man. Everything you eat, drink, wear, read—everything you use or own is taxed. You are taxed from the time you are born till you die. I do not object to taxation if it is used for the good of the country. When it is wrung out of one section of the country merely to keep another in subjection to negroes I do object to it. (Applause.) I object when it is taken from the white industrious men of the North to support the blacks and their lazy rulers in the South. (Applause.) I object to it when it is used to keep a Radical majority in power against the will of the people. I object to it when it is used by Radical electioneering agents to corrupt the electors. When it comes to honest, fair taxation for legitimate purposes, as, for instance, to pay off the national debt, palsied be my tongue before I utter a word against it. (Applause.) That national debt is now $2,700,000,000, two-thirds of that of Great Britain. We have been six years in making ours; they two hundred years in making theirs. Why in God's name are ten States kept out of the Union? Was not this immense debt incurred to keep them from going out?

Why are our national expenses—I say nothing of our local expenses—so large? In 1861, a time of peace, the cost of the army was $23,000,000. In 1868, also a time of peace, it is $83,000,000. In 1861 the navy cost $12,000,000; now it costs $31,000,000. What is it all for? We are not at war with any foreign power. We have no war among ourselves. It is done to maintain the supremacy of a party, and to prevent that glorious object, the preservation of the Union, and the authority of the Constitution, for which so many of our people sacrificed their lives. The civil expenses of the Government in 1867 were $170,000,000 more than in 1861. Do you realize the magnitude of these figures? Can you grasp them? We used to be alarmed at a debt of $70,000,000; now our civil expenses are increased to $170,000,000 in six years. What is the condition of our securities? The country is a great country. It is mighty in its agricultural and in its mineral resources, and in an energetic people; yet go into any of the European markets, and you will find United States bonds, paying six per cent. interest in gold, selling for 71 cents, while British bonds, bearing but three per cent. interest, sell for 94 cents to 95 cents. A Canadian bond pays a premium of four per cent.; a New Zealand bond is worth 109½; a Massachusetts bond 87, while the bonds of the United States are only 72. In the United States gold is at a premium of 40 per cent.; in Russia it is only 14, and in Austria 22. Is this a proper condition of things? Who is responsible? It is not the largeness of the debt; it is not that the people will not pay their taxes cheerfully; it is not that the resources of the country are not ample; but the people of the Old World, looking calmly on at us, see that we have a divided country, and that its affairs are in the hands of a partisan government bent upon power and gain, instead of being in the hands of wise statesmen and honest patriots. During the war military necessity was the excuse for everything; now it is a party necessity. Military necessity is dangerous enough, but party necessity is more dangerous still. Your duty in Connecticut is to declare in this election upon the side of a sound conservatism; to administer a rebuke to the party in power. That party will attempt to buy votes, since they cannot convince by argument. Is there a man within the sound of my voice, however poor he may be, that will sell his birth-right—who values the land of his nativity or his adoption so little as to sell his vote? The man who, in a crisis like this in the nation, would sell his vote would sell his soul. It is a poor policy to sacrifice principle for any mere personal advantage. If any man is found selling his vote, let him have the finger of scorn pointed at him forever, and go marked to his grave. In conclusion, let me say that I look for great and glorious things in Connecticut. There is no reason why you should not have them. Look at the result of the election last year; State after State declaring for the Democratic policy and against the Radical. Will you be backward now? Shall it be said that this town, which never failed before to give a Democratic majority, will fail now? I believe it will not; I trust it will not; I appeal to you to see that it does not. I appeal to you in the name of our whole country to see that Connecticut stands firm by the Union and the Constitution. You men of Connecticut are thrown to the front of the battle; see to it that your State is not false to the pledges of last spring, and that James G. English, that pure, upright, earnest, patriotic man, is not simply elected, but has a majority at least double of that you gave him last year. (Cheers.) Do that, and one thing you will accomplish, if no other: there will be no impeachment of the President, no overthrowing the Supreme Court, no forced negro suffrage; but a feeling of joy and relief will spring up among loyal men everywhere that here in the East the sun of Conservatism is rising, and an assurance that it will continue to rise until in midday splendor it shines down upon a whole people redeemed and saved from Radical misrule and Radical ruin.

CHAPTER IX.

HIS SECOND NOMINATION FOR GOVERNOR.

In the early part of the present year, when the politicians and the press throughout the country were speculating in regard to the probable nominees of the National Democratic Convention, John T.

Hoffman's name was among the foremost of those mentioned for the office of Vice-President. The circumstances connected with his official career in this city, his canvass of the State as a candidate for Governor in 1866, and the remarkable run which he made for Mayor last year, had made his name familiar to the Democracy of the country. The public judged, and wisely too, that a man who exhibited such strength and popularity among his people at home, must possess more than ordinary ability and greater elements of popularity than most men.

The Democratic press in all sections pointed to him as one of the best men that could be placed upon the national ticket for Vice-President in the event of the nominee for President coming from the West. During the time that the Chase " movement," as it was called, was talked about, the names of Chase and Hoffman were invariably mentioned together. This was so general that it was charged that the Chase " movement " meant the nomination of Mr. Hoffman as the second on the ticket, and that this was the secret of the Chase talk.

This was not the case; at least if it was, Mr. Hoffman himself had no connection with it. He declared from the outset that he did not desire the nomination for Vice-President, and could not accept it if tendered him. His ambition was to be Governor. It was towards Albany instead of Washington that his eyes were turned.

When the National Convention met, several efforts were made to make a combination with Hoffman's friends that would secure his nomination for Vice-President, with a prominent candidate in the West for President. All overtures of this kind were, however, rejected. It is not at all improbable, however, that if Senator Hendricks had received the nomination for President, Mr. Hoffman would have been compelled to yield, and to accept the second place on the ticket.

That he was looked upon as one of the most prominent men in the party on this occasion is manifested by the fact that, in the long struggle in the Convention to nominate a candidate, and numerous ballots without any result, Mr. Hoffman received the vote of one of the Western delegations on three or four ballots for President.

The moment that the National Convention adjourned, a brisk canvass sprung up in regard to the nomination for Governor. Several candidates were named as the preference of the Democracy in different parts of the State. But it was early seen that the question rested between Mr. Hoffman and Mr. Murphy of Brooklyn. The Democracy of the latter city urged the nomination of Senator Murphy with great earnestness, and his friends appointed a committee of twenty to visit different sections of the State and urge his claims upon the party. In addition to this, Senator Murphy had for several years been a member of the State Senate, and there fought the battles of the Democracy when there was not a handful of Democrats around the circle to assist him. He had in his career there won hosts of friends, and made the acquaintance of nearly all the leading politicians of the State. He had attached most of these men to him, and they now took up his cause and labored for his nomination.

As the campaign progressed, and the heated term drove many of our public men, as well as fashionable people, to the watering-places, both Mr. Hoffman and Mr. Murphy found their way to Saratoga. The large number of politicians from different sections of the State who gathered there soon commenced an active canvass of the claims and merits of the two men. It was a noticeable fact that a large majority of the politicians at Saratoga were for Mr. Murphy. This was so manifest, that his nomination over that of Mr. Hoffman was by those who looked at it from that stand-point considered a foregone conclusion. Even Mr. Murphy, relying upon the promises of those men who had always controlled their districts in the election of delegates, believed his own nomination certain.

All these miscalculated the feeling of the people. The campaign of 1866 gave Mr. Hoffman an introduction to the people of the State. When he was nominated that year for Governor they knew but little about him, except by reputation. His marked deeds in the metropolis were nearly all performed during the war, when the people throughout the State had their attention turned elsewhere. During that canvass he visited every important point in the State, and addressed a large number of meetings. This gave him an introduction to the people, and a reputation outside of the city. From that time he was recognized as something more than a local politician, and as belonging to the Democracy of the State as well as Tammany; and looked upon as one of the leaders of the Democracy of the Commonwealth. From that time they took an interest in all that he did, and watched all his movements.

Aside from all of these facts, there was a general impression that the vote of his opponent in 1866 was in some way counted larger than it really was. The mysterious way in which the returns from all the strong Republican localities were held back until the result in all the Democratic strongholds was known gave color to this supposition. There was, also, that feeling which is peculiar to the Democratic party, that when a man has made a good fight and carried their standard in its hour of adversity, to reward him when more prosperous seasons arrive. The second race of Mr. Hoffman for Mayor in New York had also aided in drawing the people throughout the State to his support.

When the primary elections were called to elect delegates to the

State Convention, a majority of those men who have controlled the
Conventions of the party for several years past were in favor of the
nomination of Henry C. Murphy. They attended the local convention with the view of either getting themselves elected delegates, or
to send men who would vote for Senator Murphy. But when they
came to meet the people at the primary election they found that they
were in earnest for Mr. Hoffman, and that they demanded his nomination. The result was that young men and new men were sent to the
State Convention. Those who had been accustomed to attend for years,
and who had been considered invincible in their own party at home,
were unable to get elected delegates wherever they had announced themselves for Murphy. Several of these men who had been for years
looked up to by their party at home, whose counsels had always
been followed and advice taken, by the rank and file, as law and gospel, were set aside in this movement, so earnest were the masses of
the party in this one direction.

All this arose from no dislike of Senator Murphy or the men who
were urging his nomination. They had their hearts set upon the
nomination of Mr. Hoffman, and were determined that there should
be no failure. Their earnestness and action in this respect were very
much like the feeling which actuated the rank and file of the Democracy in the contest which took place between the renomination of
Wm. C. Bouck and that of Silas Wright. Then the masses of the
party set aside many of the leaders, because they were pledged to
and supported Mr. Bouck, and sent new and young men to the Convention, pledged and instructed for Silas Wright. Thus it was in
this contest between Mr. Hoffman and Mr. Murphy. On almost any
other occasion they would have been delighted to follow their old
leaders in support of Senator Murphy, but as they then viewed matters they would not listen to them.

When the Convention assembled it became apparent to everybody
there that the tide was one way, that the masses of the party had
made their work sure, and that, leaving New York city out of the
question, it would be impossible to prevent the nomination of Mr.
Hoffman. Several of the old politicians of the party zealously labored
to get up a combination on some new man, and to have the names of
Hoffman and Murphy both dropped. But this move made no head-
way. Outside of the election of the delegates from the city of New
York and Brooklyn, the result of this Convention was less the work
of management and intrigue, and the nomination of Hoffman more
directly attributable to the masses of the party, than any nomination
that has taken place in this State for years.

Senator Murphy becoming convinced, after looking over the field,
that there was no chance, withdrew his name from the canvass, and

left Mr. Hoffman without a competitor when the nominations were reached in the Convention. His name was presented to the Convention by Geo. W. Miller, of Rochester, and seconded by A. Oakey Hall, of New York. The former declared, in presenting the name of Hoffman, that the people of Western New York demanded his nomination; while Mr. Hall, in seconding it, predicted that he would receive 90,000 majority in New York city. His nomination was then made by acclamation. He has accepted, and already commenced a tour of the State, addressing the people at all the principal points.

There is one peculiarity in all Mr. Hoffman's public career, and that is, the devotion of the German element of our population to him. This is seen at all their political gatherings, and without distinction of party predilection among them.

CHAPTER X.

JOHN T. HOFFMAN AS A MAN AND ORATOR.

The public and private character of John T. Hoffman is unassailable. His bitterest enemies have never dared to impugn his private character; none have ever questioned his public acts, except those who have failed to use him to aid their corrupt schemes. The support of the newspaper which has assailed him the most was promised him by an agent, who pretended that he had authority to speak, if he would favor a scheme which the owner of that journal desired, and the threat of its opposition made if he refused. All this had no effect upon Mr. Hoffman. He acted on that question, as on all others, in accordance with what he conscientiously believed to be the interests of the people, and let the consequences take care of themselves. This has, in fact, always been his guide in official life: to perform his duty conscientiously, administer the trusts placed in his hands in a manner that would best subserve the interests of the people, without stopping to consider whether it will affect his popularity or not.

He is a man of simple tastes and temperate living; a cultured Christian gentleman, of domestic habits, spending most of his leisure hours with his family.

There is an impression existing to a great extent that he is aristocratic, in the sense which is best expressed in the homely phrase, "stuck up." But this is far from the case. He is a man, in many respects, reserved; his poor health in early life necessarily led him into different habits and created different tastes from those which characterize most of our public men of the day. That apparent haughtiness in his manner all disappears upon acquaintance, and the man who seemed aristocratic at first sight becomes genial, warm, and companionable.

He is becoming one of the most popular speakers of the day. His style is different from that of Seymour, Pendleton, Church, and many other prominent public speakers of the times. It is, however, fully as attractive as either, except it may be that of Seymour. His speeches are extemporaneous, neither written out beforehand nor committed to memory.

His arguments are always cogent and to the point, his illustrations instructive, his language faultless, his words impressive, while his perorations have an inspiriting effect upon the audience.

His independent and patriotic course as Recorder of this city, the unflinching manner in which he dealt out justice to all classes of offenders against the law, the vigilance with which he has guarded the public interests, and the promptitude with which he has vetoed all corrupt or questionable projects since he has been Mayor, furnish unmistakable evidence of his fitness for the position for which he is now a candidate. It further proves that the affairs of the State can be safely placed in his hands.

ALLEN C. BEACH.

HIS BOYHOOD STRUGGLES.

The Democratic nominee for Lieutenant Governor, ALLEN C. BEACH, is in every respect a self-made man, and comes from New England stock. His grandfather was a native of Connecticut and his grandmother of Massachusetts. His father was born in Montgomery county, while his mother is a native of Herkimer county of this State.

The father of Mr. Beach has long been well known to the people in Montgomery, Herkimer, and Madison counties, where he has for over thirty years been stationed as minister of the gospel. He is a clergyman in the Baptist Church, and has spent his life preaching in the small towns in those counties mentioned, and is now, at an advanced age, residing at Hamilton, Madison county.

The calling of a minister in the rural towns is not generally lucrative. Those who accept that mission in the country have found it hard work and poor pay. Rev. Mr. Beach's experience during the early portion of his ministerial life was no exception to this rule. He was stationed at Fairfield, Herkimer county, when the subject of this biography was born.

ALLEN C. BEACH was born on the 9th day of October, 1825. He received such education as the limited means of his father and a village school at that time furnished, until he reached the age of twelve years; at that age he left home and commenced to take care of himself. This was early to leave the parental roof, and commence to fight the battles of life. But young Beach, seeing the necessity, had the courage and fortitude even at that age to meet it. He first obtained work on a farm, where he remained for three years. During this time his leisure hours were spent in studying, and he was often known to go a great distance after the close of his day's work to obtain books to read and study—thus surmounting difficulties to obtain knowledge and better his condition, such as but few youths of this day would think of meeting.

In this manner he fitted himself for teaching school, and at the end of three years' service on the farm, before he was sixteen years old, he commenced teaching in a district school during the winter months. His thirst for knowledge grew with his years, and his determination to obtain a thorough education now became the ambition of his life. With the money that he earned teaching during the winter months, he clothed himself and paid his way at an academy during the summer. His first summer, after he had decided upon this course, was spent at the Jordan Academy, Onondaga county. As soon as the time arrived for the commencement of the winter schools he returned to his task, spending the winter in teaching and studying, making in this manner greater progress than most youths do whose parents are able to keep them constantly at school.

Several years were spent by Mr. Beach in this way, alternating between teaching and studying. After the second year he attended, during the summer months, the academy at Mexico, Oswego county, and there fitted himself for college. By practising economy and carefully husbanding his earnings, he had managed, when he reached the age of twenty-one, to save enough to enable him to enter college.

It may be considered a remarkable coincidence that Mr. Beach entered Union College in 1846, the same year and just about the same time that John T. Hoffman received his diploma as a graduate in the same college ; the nominee for Governor passing out of one door with his diploma, while the candidate on the same ticket for Lieutenant-Governor was entering another door to commence the struggle for the same prize.

The same habits of industry and hard study which had characterized Mr. Beach while preparing himself for college, were continued during his term there. As might be expected, he made rapid progress, and in 1848 he graduated, receiving among the highest honors of his class.

He found by this time that his means were exhausted and his savings all vanished. But he had the consolation of knowing that they had been wisely spent and that he had been benefited by it. But he was compelled to immediately obtain a position where he could again replenish his purse.

On leaving college he obtained a situation as one of the assistants in the Watertown Academy. While discharging the duties of that position, he commenced studying law with the late Joshua Moore, one of the leading barristers of that section of the State. He pursued these studies, alternating between teaching and reading law, for some four years, and was admitted to the bar in 1852. At the death of

Mr. Moore he formed a partnership with Levi H. Brown, and has been associated with him ever since 1854. The firm of Brown & Beach has, for a number of years, stood foremost among the legal firms in Northern New York, and they are considered the leading men at the bar in Jefferson county.

About one year after he was admitted to the bar, or in 1853, Mr. Beach married the daughter of Norris M. Woodruff, of Watertown, one of the principal families in that section. This union was not of long duration; in 1856 the wife was stricken down with disease and died. Mr. Beach remained a widower until 1862, when he was again married, this time to Mrs. Pickering, of Saratoga Springs.

Mr. Beach was a delegate to the National Convention at Charleston in 1860, and was an ardent supporter of Stephen A. Douglas, both at the Charleston and Baltimore meetings of that Convention. He has been Chairman of the Democratic County Committee on several occasions, and in this capacity has exhibited great organizing ability.

In 1863 he was nominated by the Democracy of his county for County Judge. He ran ahead of his ticket, but the county was then some three thousand Republican—too much to overcome. He was last year nominated as a delegate to the Constitutional Convention, and came within four hundred votes of carrying his county, which was at the previous election some 2,800 Republican, showing that he possesses the elements of popularity, and is strong where he is well known.

The Democracy of Jefferson county have frequently sent him as a delegate to the State Convention, where he has taken an active part. He was also a delegate to the National Convention which met in New York on the 4th of July last.

He has accumulated a moderate competency in the practice of his profession, is a man of fine legal attainments, a ripe scholar, a man of strict integrity, and, as we have already shown, belongs to that class of men who have worked their way upward in spite of adverse circumstances.

He has at all times thoroughly identified himself with the local interests of his town, and more especially has he taken a deep interest in educational matters, and is at the present time President of the Board of Education of Watertown.

He is also a man of fine personal appearance—large frame, manly form, light complexion, dark hair and eyes, smoothly shaven except a moustache, is stoutly built, being six feet high and weighing two hundred and twenty-five pounds.

In 1863, during the period when there was so much excitement over the arrest of individuals, and their incarceration in prisons without trial, Mr. Beach, at the request of many of the leading citizens, delivered a speech at Rutland, Jefferson county, which has been since largely quoted from, and pronounced by some of the ablest jurists in the State a masterly document. The following are some of the points of this speech:

The privilege of the writ of habeas corpus is not appreciated or understood in the United States as it is in England, for the reason that we have never had, until within the last three years, any serious contest for that right. It has been as free, within certain well-defined legal restrictions, as air, and it is difficult for the people to believe, without experience, that they are to be or can be arbitrarily and illegally deprived of the one any more than the other.

DEFINITION AND EXPLANATION OF HABEAS CORPUS.

" *Habeas corpus* " are two Latin words, meaning " have the body," and the writ happens to have that name from the circumstance that formerly in England all writs were written in Latin and received the name of the first or most prominent words in them.

You are a law-abiding citizen, but without any process of law you are arrested and imprisoned. What instrumentality does the law provide for your release from such imprisonment? Only the habeas corpus.

Upon a petition stating the facts entitling you to it, you or your friends or agent applies to a judge or court of record for a writ of habeas corpus; the court or judge issues the writ, directed to the person detaining you, and commanding him to " have the body " of the person restrained in his liberty before such judge or court at the time named in the writ. Thus you are brought up before the judge, and the cause of your detention is investigated. If you are legally held you cannot be discharged, but must be remanded into custody. If illegally held you must be discharged, and thus is your right to personal liberty maintained. None but the innocent can be released by it. Hence it is the writ for the protection and security of the innocent. It is the GREAT WRIT OF FREEDOM.

The Anglo-Saxon is jealous of any encroachment upon his liberty. He spurns the manacles of slavery, and resists every attempt of power to subject him to illegal restraint. Hence we find an almost continual struggle between the monarchs and the people of England for hundreds of years—on the one hand to maintain, and on the other to overthrow the power of arresting and imprisoning the citizens at will. Even after the Barons of England had wrested from King John " *Magna Charta*," in the year 1215, he as well as subsequent kings of England attempted to nullify its benefits and deny them to the people. The contest between the executive and the people was renewed at various times, until finally the people triumphed, and for the last two hundred years it has been the settled and agreed law of England that every Englishman restrained of his liberty shall have the privilege of a writ of habeas corpus, and that the same shall in no case be suspended by the executive. An entry on the Journal of the House of Commons, made on the 3d day of April, 1628, reads as follows: " Resolved upon question, that the writ of habeas corpus may not be denied, but ought to be granted, to every man that is committed or detained in prison or otherwise restrained, *though it be by the* COMMAND OF THE KING, *the Privy Council, or any other,* he praying the same. Passed without negative."

We also find on the Journal of the House of Lords this entry, made in 1704:

" *Resolved*, That every Englishman who is imprisoned by *any authority whatso-ever*, has an undoubted right by his agents or friends to apply for and obtain a writ of habeas corpus in order to procure his liberty by due course of law ;" and again in the same year it was said by the House of Lords with greater distinct-ness : "It has been allowed by the known common law, it is the right of every subject under restraint, upon demand, to have the writ of habeas corpus, and thereupon to be brought before some proper court where it may be examined whether he be detained for lawful cause."

For more than two hundred years, no monarch of England has attempt-ed to suspend the habeas corpus. For more than two hundred years, it would have cost any King of England his crown, if he had dared to exercise such power.

The American Colonies were formed mostly by emigrants from England, and were subjects of the British crown. Hence the common law of England, includ-ing the right to do process of law and the writ of habeas corpus as understood and enjoyed in England, was in force in this country at the time of the Revolu-tion ; accordingly when our fathers framed the Constitution, they did not origi-nate or ordain those great rights. They speak of them as well understood facts, and only allude to the habeas corpus in the Constitution in connection with a provision limiting the power of Congress to suspend it. Constitution, Art. 1, sec. 9. In England, only Parliament can suspend it, and that only for a limited and specified period. In the United States, only Congress can exercise that power, and that, too, is limited to cases of invasion and rebellion when the public safety requires it.

It was never claimed that the President could legally suspend the writ until the year 1861.

When it is considered that this Palladium of our liberties was wrested from executive power, it will be seen how absurd is the idea that the people would intrust it to the safe-keeping of the executive, or allow it to be even tempo-rarily suspended by any power other than their immediate representatives in Congress assembled.

In the war of 1812, there was far more opposition to the war and to the administration than there is now.

In the war with Mexico, one of the great political parties of that time was an avowed peace party, denounced the war, and did all in its power to embarrass the Administration.

In the Shay insurrection, the whiskey rebellion, and the Dorr rebellion, we had armed rebels within our own Northern States. Yet in no one of those wars or insurrections was the habeas corpus suspended ; much less was it suggested that the President ought to or could exercise that power.

During the progress of the famous Burr conspiracy, Mr. Jefferson, who was then President, communicated to the Senate the fact that a man arrested for treason had been released on habeas corpus. The Senate thereupon passed a bill suspending the writ, and sent it to the House, but the House immediately rejected it by an almost unanimous vote.

This is the only case in which Congress attempted to exercise the power of suspension, and this, as we have seen, failed.

THE CONSTITUTION.

The Constitution was framed by delegates appointed by the States, and was adopted by the people of the States. The Federal Government has no existence outside of the Constitution. It never would have existed unless created by the

7

States, and has therefore just so much, and no more, power than its creators, the States, gave it. Any exercise of power by the Federal Government, not granted and delegated to it by the people of the several States in the Constitution, is usurpation. But the Constitution does not delegate to the President power to suspend the *habeas corpus*. How, then, can he rightfully suspend it any more than you or I?

The Constitution (Article 10, Amendments) also expressly states that " The powers not delegated to the United States by the Constitution, nor prohibited by it to the States, are reserved to the States respectively, or to the people."

" Being an instrument of limited and enumerated powers, it follows irresistibly that what is not conferred is withheld, and belongs to the State authorities, if invested by their constitutions of government respectively in them; and if not so invested. it is retained by the people as a part of their residuary sovereignty." (Abridgment, Story's Com. on Const., p. 712.)

WHAT THE COURT SAYS.

Chief-Justice Marshall, delivering the opinion of the Supreme Court in the cases of Bollman and Swartout (4 Cranch, 101), says: " If at any time the public safety should require the suspension of the powers vested by this (the *habeas corpus*) act in the Courts of the United States, *it is for the Legislature to say so.* That question depends on political considerations, on which the Legislature is to decide. Until the legislative will be expressed, this Court can only see its duty, and must obey the laws." The Chief-Justice of the United States, in his opinion in the Merryman case in 1861 (9 Am. Law Reg., 524-530), says: " He (the President) certainly does not faithfully execute the laws if he takes upon himself *legislative power by suspending the writ of habeas corpus,*" thus expressly deciding that the act of suspending the *habeas corpus* is the exercise of legislative powers.

THE POWER USURPED BY MR. LINCOLN.

Violent hands were first laid upon this safeguard of liberty, in 1861, by President Lincoln. *He* first assumed the power to arrest the citizen without due or any process of law—to convey the victim within some Government fortress, or guard him by a military force too strong to be overcome by the officers of the law, and to set at defiance the law he had just solemnly sworn to see executed and enforced, and the Constitution he had sworn to protect and defend.

In 1862, Congress, a majority of which were his pliant tools, pretended to enact a law delegating to the President power to suspend the writ of habeas corpus in the peaceful and law-abiding States of the Union, without any restriction or limitation as to time or place, except his judgment.

Laws of the United States passed 1862, chap. 81, sec. 1.

Accordingly the President did, on the 15th day of September, 1863, issue his proclamation, in which he declared the writ suspended.

The able and eminent lawyers of the Republican party preserve an ominous silence. But now, as ever, there are found minions of power ready to justify any atrocity. Let us then examine the question. The proposition is, that one department of Government may legally delegate the exercise of its peculiar functions to another department.

CANNOT BE DELEGATED.

It would seem that the bare statement of the proposition was its best refutation. The Constitution creates three separate departments of Government—a legislative, a judicial, and an executive.

It delegates to the legislative department power to pass laws; to the judicial, power to expound and adjudicate; and to the President, executive power.

The Constitution defines and limits the powers and duties of each department. Neither department has any other or greater powers than are delegated to it by the Constitution.

The Constitution does not delegate to any department the right or power to exercise the powers, or discharge the duties, of any other department.

Hence the President has no more right to discharge the duties or exercise the powers of Congress, than Congress has to make legal adjudications, or than Courts have to exercise the pardoning power. It follows, therefore, that Congress cannot delegate to the President, and he cannot exercise, the power to suspend the habeas corpus.

The Constitution of the United States provides (Article 1, Sec. 1) as follows:

"All legislative powers herein granted shall be vested in a Congress of the United States, which shall consist of a Senate and House of Representatives."

The Constitution of the State of New York provides (Article 3, Sec. 1) as follows:

"The legislative powers of this State shall be vested in a Senate and Assembly."

So that by the Constitutions of this State and the United States, legislative powers are vested in and restricted to the legislative department.

DECISIONS OF THE COURTS.

On the 26th day of March, 1849, the Legislature of this State attempted to violate this principle, by passing an act to establish free schools in this State, and referring to the electors of the State the question whether that act should become a law. The General Terms of the 2d and of the 5th Districts decided that the act was unconstitutional and void, and that the electors had no power to determine that question, and the Court of Appeals of this State affirmed both of those judgments.

Judge Barculo, in pronouncing the opinion of the Court in one of those cases, says (15 Barb. 115, 116): "Upon what principle, then, can the representative transfer to any other person or persons the power of making, or, what is tantamount, the power of breathing life and efficacy into laws? Suppose they should attempt to clothe with this authority some individual, as the Governor or Attorney-General, would not the common-sense of the whole community be shocked at their dereliction of duty?

"And above all, he cannot delegate to others the trust which has been expressly confided in him.

"*Delegata potestas non potest delegati.* Delegated power cannot be delegated, is a settled maxim of common law, in full force at the present day, and never more applicable than to the case of a legislator."

In the opinion of the Court in the case in the 5th District (15 Barb. 128), which Court was composed of Judges Gridley, W. F. Allen, Pratt, and Hubbard, it is said by Judge Pratt, in delivering the unanimous opinion of the Court:

"It is a well-settled principle that when a trust or confidence is confided to any person or class of persons, the trustees cannot delegate the trust. And what trust, what confidence, is more sacred, more responsible, than the power to make the laws of a free people? Upon the same question in the Court of Appeals, the Court say (4 Selden, 491): "The Legislature has no power to make a statute dependent on such a contingency, because it would be confiding to others that legislative discretion which they are bound to exercise themselves, and which they cannot delegate or commit to any other man or men to be exercised." The same principle has been recognized and upheld in the highest courts of Pennsylvania and of Delaware. (6 Barr, 507.) Rice *v.* Foster (4 Harrington, 479).

And the Supreme Court of the United States decided in Hayburn's case (2 Dallas, 406–410. and Notes) that Congress has no constitutional power to impose on judicial officers any duties that are not strictly judicial.

Judge Story, in his Commentaries on the Constitution (Abridgment, p. 483, sec. 676), says: " It would seem, as the power is given to Congress to suspend the writ of habeas corpus in cases of rebellion or invasion, that the right to judge whether the exigency had arisen must exclusively belong to that body." (Congress.)

But it is said that it is a military necessity—that the President should exercise these extraordinary powers. We can see no good, but great evil, as the result. There is no rebellion or invasion in the State of New York, and no resistance to the Courts, or their process, by any man or set of men *except the Administration.* No party in the Northern States proposes peace while the rebels are in arms. What, then, does divide the people ? Nothing but the unwise and unnecessary persistence of the Administration in violating the Constitution. The people are alarmed at such unwarranted exercise of power, and justly fear that it will grow into a precedent.

The language of all our great and good men has been uniform upon this point. Judge Bronson says (3 Comstock, 568): " There is always some plausible reason for the latitudinarian constructions which are resorted to for the purpose of acquiring power ; some evil to be averted, or good to be attained, by pushing the powers of the Government beyond their legitimate boundary. It is by yielding to such influences that Constitutions are gradually undermined and finally overthrown. . . . One step taken by the Legislature or the judiciary in enlarging the powers of the Government opens the door for another, which will be sure to follow, and so the process goes on until all respect for the fundamental law is lost, and the powers of the government are just what those in authority please to call them." Mr. Justice Story, one of the most eminent jurists of the age, and one of the ablest judges of the United States Court, in his Commentaries on the Constitution (Abridgment, page 713) says : " What is to become of constitutions of government if they are to rest, not upon the plain import of their words, but upon conjectural enlargements and restrictions to suit the temporary passions and interests of the day ? Let us never forget that our constitutions of government are solemn instruments addressed to the common-sense of the people, and designed to fix and perpetuate their rights and liberties. They are not to be frittered away to please the demagogues of the day. They are not to be violated to gratify the ambition of political leaders ; they are to speak in the same voice now and forever ; they are of no man's private interpretation. They are ordained by the will of the people ; and can be changed only by the sovereign command of the people."

That sounds very much like the speeches of Governor Seymour, and yet, for so talking, he is branded as a traitor.

Hear also what the Father of his Country said in that immortal address which seems almost to be imbued with the spirit of prophecy. He says: " It is important likewise that the habits of thinking in a free country should inspire caution in those intrusted with its administration to confine themselves within their respective constitutional spheres, avoiding in the exercise of the power of one department to encroach upon another. The spirit of encroachment tends to consolidate the powers of all the departments in one, and thus to create, whatever the form of the government, a real despotism. A just estimate of that love of power and proneness to abuse it which predominate in the human heart, is sufficient to satisfy us of the truth of this position. The necessity of reciprocal checks in the exercise of political power, by dividing and distributing it into different depositories, and constituting each the guardian of the public weal against invasion of the others, has been evinced by experiments ancient and modern ; some of them in our own country and under our own eyes.

"To preserve them must be as necessary as to institute them. If, in the opinion of the people, the distribution or modification of the constitutional powers be in any particular wrong, let it be corrected by an amendment in the way which the Constitution designated. BUT LET THERE BE NO CHANGE BY USURPATION ; for though this may in one instance be the instrument of good, it is the customary weapon by which free governments are destroyed. The precedent must always greatly overbalance in permanent evil any partial or transient benefit which the use can at any time yield."

Washington made no reservation in favor of times of war or of military necessity, though he had recently conducted the country through a seven years' war, one of the most difficult and desperate recorded in history.

Is it not too plain for controversy ; is it not established by history, by the Constitution, by the uniform practice of the government, by the decisions of the courts, and by the opinions of our ablest and best jurists and statesmen, that the habeas corpus is not and cannot be thus suspended ; that the exercise of that power without right, by the President, is a "change by usurpation," a denial of a plain constitutional right ? President Lincoln, in his inaugural, pronounces the following judgment against himself and his party. He says : "Happily, the human mind is so constituted that no party can reach the audacity of denying any right plainly written in the Constitution. If, by mere force of numbers, a majority should deprive a minority of any clearly written constitutional right, it might in a moral point of view justify revolution."

If power has made such immense strides over constitutional rights in two years, what are we to expect if we tamely submit to its continuance in that course in the indefinite future ?

But it is said we should not embarrass the Government by raising such questions. The government of the Constitution is the only government we can recognize. Any other is a usurpation, and not a government ; and we have the right to, and do say to the Administration—Do not *you* embarrass the true men of the North, the Government and yourselves, by insisting upon the suspension and overthrow of our rights under any pretext whatever ?

But they say, let us put down the rebellion first, and then we will talk of these questions. We, too, say put down the rebellion ; and we say it never can be put down by putting down the rights and liberties of loyal men. It is because we wish the rebellion put down, and the good old Union restored, that we implore the Administration and its friends not to take a course which must divide the North, unite the South, and make it doubtful whether the end will not be the subversion of constitutional government and the destruction of that right most sacred to every American citizen—liberty regulated by law.

Mr. Beach's name was first mentioned for the position of Lieutenant-Governor soon after the adjournment of the National Democratic Convention. It was first brought out in the political columns of the

New York *World*. This caused an inquiry in regard to his abilities and character, which resulted in securing for him advocates among those who had prior to this been entire strangers to him.

As the delegates gathered at the Albany Convention, and were introduced to Mr. Beach, they became impressed with his manners and general bearing, while his universal reputation as a man of the strictest probity and high moral character gained him friends everywhere.

There were three candidates for this position in the Convention; Allen C. Beach, A. P. Lanning, and Wm. J. Averill. It is generally supposed that Mr. Beach owed his nomination to the attack made upon his opponents, and the charges that were made that Mr. Lanning had entered into league with Tammany. All these "exposures" by the enthusiastic and imaginative gentlemen from Kings may have hastened the nomination of Mr. Beach, but it did not change the result. Long before the balloting was reached, it was just as apparent as anything could be, that a majority of the Convention preferred Mr. Beach to either of the other candidates. It was also equally certain, that whenever there was any break in the supporters of either of the other candidates, they would go to Mr. Beach. The flurry in the Convention may have brought about the nomination one ballot sooner than it would, had not the attack been made.

As it was, the nomination was made on the first ballot, the vote standing as follows:

A. C. Beach............................68
A. P. Lanning..........................47
W. J. Averill.......................... 9

On the announcement of the result, Mr. Beach was loudly called for, and went forward and briefly addressed the Convention; thanking them for the honor, the confidence and partiality they had shown him in giving him the nomination, and promised to do all in his power to advance the principles and interests of the Democratic party.

On his arrival home, after the close of the proceedings of the Convention, he was met at the depot by a large number of citizens of Watertown, who gathered there, irrespective of party, to welcome him. An address of welcome was delivered by James F. Starbuck, to which Mr. Beach briefly responded:

CITIZENS OF WATERTOWN:—I thank you for this spontaneous expression of your kindness. I can find no fitting words in which to tell you how deeply I am affected by it and by the very flattering terms in which you have been pleased to convey that expression through the eloquent and esteemed fellow-citizen who has spoken in your behalf. I came among you nearly twenty years ago, a stranger to you all. Through all those long years you have treated me with uniform kindness and consideration. Ever since my name was first publicly mentioned in connection with the office to which I have been nominated, it has been the hope and the wish, I believe, of all the citizens of Watertown that I should receive that nomination. At the Convention, every man who was there from Jefferson county, as well as a host of warm-hearted friends from other counties, labored in my behalf with the real enthusiasm of brothers; and never, never while my memory remains, can I forget their devotion to me. Fellow-citizens, I never cast a vote anywhere except in Watertown. Of all people in the world, therefore, you best know my political record; whether it is an honest one I leave to your judgment, and by that judgment I will cheerfully abide. The present condition of our country is certainly not a happy one. Immense burdens of debt and taxation are resting with crushing weight upon the productive industry of our land. The relations of the States of our Union to each other and to the general Government, all concede are not what they should be. Let us, then, laying aside all passion, prejudice, and partisanship, endeavor to ascertain and adopt the wisest and surest means of restoring our beloved country to a condition of peace and prosperity. Again thanking you for this manifestation of your good-will, I wish you a very good-night.

Mr. Beach's brief address was received with rounds of applause, and the affair terminated greatly to the satisfaction of all who participated.

There is a pleasure in tracing the career of men who have marched steadily onward from obscure positions in boyhood to those of influence, prominence, and high trusts when they approach the prime of life. There is something grand in the course of a man who has chosen the undeviating line of rectitude, has selected for himself an honorable position in society as his aim, and steadily moves forward in spite of all obstacles, unaided and alone, accomplishing that aim, and reaching such a prominence that the people are glad to select him as their representative. Such a man is Allen C. Beach. Of humble parentage, he has made for himself a name and reputation to be envied, has struggled against adversity, educated himself, and has outstripped in the race for honors most of those who had all the appliances of wealth and influence to aid them. He is one of that class of men who work their way up in spite of adverse circumstances. There is about his history and his early career much that sounds like real romance, and many of those traits of character which stood forth so prominently in Franklin and other self-made men in the early days of our Republic. A study of his early life instinctively draws a person to him, and wherever his traits of character are known they cannot fail to be admired. With all his energy, his industry, his integrity, and his great moral worth, he is a man of great modesty, and shows an entire absence of arrogance in his nature.

Mr. Beach has been for years prominently connected with the Masonic Order at Watertown, and for some time at the head of the Chapter. He has in this connection received higher honors from the people of his own town than any other person connected with the Masonic fraternity at that place.

OLIVER BASCOM.

THE Democratic nominee for Canal Commissioner, Mr. Bascom, is a native of the State of Vermont, and was born in 1815. But he acted on the idea that Vermont is a good State to be born in, but a better State to emigrate from. His parents left that State when he was but ten years old, and took up their residence in Washington county.

Mr. Bascom is a man who has carved his own fortune. He commenced life as a clerk in the mercantile business, and was afterwards in a transportation house. In 1841 he began business for himself, in the transportation and forwarding line, for which his term as clerk had specially fitted him. In 1851 he entered into a partnership, and formed the firm of Bascom, Vaughn & Co. This house met with remarkable success, and in 1857 the business which it had obtained became so extensive that the firm was made the nucleus of the Northern Transportation Company. Mr. Bascom was the secretary and treasurer of this company until 1862, when he temporarily retired and spent a short time in California. The success of this company is far beyond that of any other that has been organized, the dividends reaching from 20 to 25 per cent. Its prosperity is in a great measure attributed to the ability and sagacity of Mr. Bascom.

Since his return from California, he has been engaged in farming and in the lumber trade, and is one of the most successful business men in his section of the State. Everything that he has undertaken in his life has been successful, and he is in every way qualified for the duties which the Democracy propose to place in his hands. In his long business career and extensive dealings he has kept his name without the least stain upon it.

His business called his attention directly to the condition and the wants of the canals. His knowledge on this point is practical, and it was for this reason that his nomination was pressed. His nomination at the Convention was opposed by the "Canal Ring," but earnestly urged by the business men of North-eastern New York.

Mr. Bascom is now fifty-three years of age. He cast his first vote, on arriving at his majority, for the Democratic ticket, and has never voted any other. He did not seek this nomination, but it was urged upon him, because of his peculiar fitness for the office.

During the days of the Whig party, his town in Washington county gave 400 Whig majority, and yet he was nominated and elected Supervisor, overcoming by his personal popularity that majority. When he first moved to Whitehall, there were only fifty Democrats in the town, to three hundred and fifty Opposition. He has managed, since the commencement of the war, to turn it around to a Democratic town. He was twice elected Supervisor during the war, and was chairman of the committee to raise the money necessary to enable his town to fill the quota. In fact he had the entire responsibility of filling the quota on his shoulders. He has been four times elected Supervisor, running against Whig candidates in 1851 and 1852, and against Republicans in 1863 and 1864. He ran for Assembly a year or two since, and carried his own town by 400 majority, receiving 600 votes out of the 800 polled in the town.

He received the nomination for Canal Commissioner on the first ballot, and that, too, against the opposition of what is known as the Canal Ring. He was last year prominently mentioned in the State Convention for the office of State Treasurer.

DAVID B. MᶜNEIL.

ALL of those politicians who have any recollection of the public men in this State, and possess any knowledge of the *personnel* of politics of New York during the two terms that Andrew Jackson was President, will remember Col. D. B. McNeil, of Northern New York. He was a great favorite of General Jackson, a warm personal friend of Silas Wright, and for a long time one of the most prominent and influential politicians in North-eastern New York; was appointed by Jackson, Collector of the Port of Plattsburgh during his first term as President, and reappointed at the commencement of the second term. He was, in fact, one of those men of strict integrity and unflinching honesty whom Jackson delighted to favor.

This gentleman was the father of the present Democratic candidate for State Prison Inspector, David B. McNeil, who was called junior until the death of the elder McNeil, within the last three or four years. He was born in Essex county, in this State, in 1818, and is therefore only three years younger than the nominee for Canal Commissioner.

In his boyhood days he saw many of the leading Democratic politicians and statesmen of this State. All who passed through that section invariably stopped at his father's house and talked over the affairs of the country. He also had instilled in him those precepts and those ideas of political responsibilities and rectitude which should be exercised by officials, but which, alas! but too few of our office-holders of the present time recognize.

He was educated at the Plattsburgh Academy, and fitted for the mercantile business. He was not very successful in this line, and was appointed invoice-clerk in the New York Custom-house by Van Ness, and continued in the same capacity through the administration of that office by Cornelius W. Lawrence. Soon after he left the Custom-house, he was made clerk at the Clinton Prison, a highly responsible position, which he held for seven years. He was subsequently five years in the Secretary of State's office, having been called into service by D. R. Floyd Jones, and retained by his successor. Leaving the Secretary of State's office, he was appointed warden of the Auburn

Prison, a position that he held sixteen months, when the Radicals obtaining the power, turned him out.

One of the most striking characteristics of his career as warden of that prison is found fully set forth in the Prison Reports to the Legislature, where it is shown that under his management of the work, in the contracts for supplies, and the work of the men, he made the prison pay, during the last fiscal year in which he had charge, $16,000 over and above all expenses. The Radicals coming into power, turned him out of office ; and his Radical successor, during the very next year, run the prison behind $40,000. Under McNeil, it paid $16,000 in one year to the State. Under his Radical successor, it cost the State $40,000 the very next year, a difference of $56,000 in one year in favor of McNeil's management. McNeil came out of office poor. As to his successor in that respect, we leave the matter to general rumor. One worked for the State as zealously and faithfully as he would have watched his own business, and great saving was the result.

Mr. McNeil was nominated for State Prison Inspector in 1863, and again in 1864. He has stood with the Democracy as one of their faithful sentinels on the tower during the days of adversity, and they now propose to reward him. There is no man in the State whose experience has given him such an insight into the workings of our prisons, or who practically knows so well as he the wants of the prisons, and how they can be conducted so as to best subserve the interests of the State.

Mr. McNeil is one of those conscientious men who are honest by education, by principle, and by practice, and one whom no amount of temptation would swerve from his line of duty, or cause him to deviate a hair's breadth from official rectitude. There are too few men of that class in public life at the present time for the people to let the opportunity of selecting one go by. Were our offices all filled by men of his probity, our taxes would be less, the National debt would be on the decrease instead of increase, our currency would be equal to gold in value, and our government securities would not be hawked around the markets of Europe at a less price than is paid for those of Brazil or the Sick Man of the East.

EDWIN OSCAR PERRIN.

THE Democratic nominee for Clerk of the Court of Appeals, Edwin Oscar Perrin, was born at Springfield, Ohio, in 1822. His father was the Hon. Joseph Perrin, for a long time Judge of the Circuit Court of that district, and a Whig politician of considerable note. Joseph Perrin was a native of Maryland, moved to Kentucky, and there married a daughter of Maddox Fisher, of Lexington, and soon after moved to Springfield, Ohio. His father-in-law, or the maternal grandfather of the subject of this biography, inherited a large number of slaves; and soon after the removal of the elder Perrin to Springfield, Mr. Fisher followed, taking with him his slaves, and giving them their freedom on arriving there.

Edwin Oscar Perrin, the subject of this sketch, was educated at the Springfield Academy, and studied law with the Hon. Samson Mason, who was member of Congress from that district for four or five terms.

Young Perrin was admitted to the bar in 1842, when but twenty years of age, and during the following year removed to Memphis, Tennessee, where he entered upon the practice of his profession. He was reared and educated as a Whig. At the commencement of General Taylor's administration he was appointed Navy Agent and Purser of the Memphis Navy Yard, and held the position until the inauguration of Franklin Pierce. He then formed a partnership with a law firm at Memphis, and in 1854 came to New York city, to open a branch office, the firm having entered extensively upon the business of making Southern collections for Northern merchants. The war coming on in 1861, broke up the business, when Mr. Perrin dissolved his connection with the Memphis firm, and remained North.

In 1857 Mr. Perrin accompanied Gov. Robt. J. Walker to Kansas, and stumped the Territory with him against the Lecompton Constitution. On his return from Kansas he was twice nominated for

Assembly in Brooklyn, and defeated each time, owing to a split in the party, and two candidates running on one side. Immediately after the war broke out he was sent by Secretary Cameron, then in charge of the War Department, on a confidential mission to New Mexico, then being invaded by the rebels under General Sibley, and was with Kit Carson and his command during the latter part of 1861 and part of 1862. Col. Carson paid him a high tribute for his fidelity and courage during that campaign. In a letter which he wrote to a Senator at Washington, Col. Carson, after reciting the risks and exposures which Mr. Perrin underwent in order to supply our troops with food, clothing, and equipments, and saying that "Mr. Perrin ran fifty chances of being scalped where he did one of escape in his journeyings through that country where they both were stationed, swarming as it was with savage Indians and hostile rebels," says :

If such voluntary exposures to danger, and such sacrifices for the cause of the country, is not sufficient proof of loyalty, fidelity, and devotion, nothing I can add will strengthen it. I repeat that no man in New Mexico ever questioned his courage and fidelity.

Yours, very respectfully,

C. CARSON,
Late Col. Commanding.

In the days of the Whig party he was always to be found on the stump during every canvass, and spoke side by side with such orators as James C. Jones, Meredith P. Gentry, Neil S. Brown, of Tennessee, and Tom Corwin, of Ohio, and stumped this State for Fillmore in 1856.

He has been Secretary of a number of the State Conventions of the Democracy; was a delegate to, and Secretary of, the Philadelphia Johnson Convention in 1866. Soon after the adjournment of that Convention he was appointed Assessor for the First District of this State, but the Senate refused to confirm his appointment. Subsequently he was appointed by President Johnson Chief-Justice of the Supreme Court of Utah, and the Senate again rejected his nomination. He ran for the same office for which he is now nominated, three years ago.

He has been selected the Secretary of four National Democratic Conventions, and his voice has been heard from the platform of every Democratic State Convention that has been held of late years; and he has stumped the State in every recent campaign, stumping Maine with Douglas in 1860.

He is a good speaker, and has been generally useful to the party.

www.ingramcontent.com/pod-product-compliance
Lightning Source LLC
Chambersburg PA
CBHW022142020726
47496CB00008B/2512